Legend Days

Also by Jamake Highwater

Jamake Highwater

Legend Days

PART ONE OF

The Ghost Horse Cycle

Harper & Row, Publishers

NEW YORK

Library of Congress Cataloging in Publication Data
Highwater, Jamake.
  Legend days.

  "A Charlotte Zolotow book"—Half t.p.
  Summary: Abandoned in the wilderness after smallpox
devastates her tribe, eleven-year-old Amana acquires from
Grandfather Fox a warrior's courage and a hunter's
prowess, gifts that sustain her as she watches the
progressive disintegration of her people.
  1. Indians of North America—Juvenile fiction.
[1. Indians of North America—Fiction]   I. Title.
PZ7.H5443Le 1984   [Fic]   82-48852
ISBN 0-06-022303-0
ISBN 0-06-022304-9 (lib. bdg.)

Designed by Constance Fogler
1 2 3 4 5 6 7 8 9 10
First Edition

For Ed Calf Robe

SPIRITUAL FATHER
WHO GAVE ME MY NAME

The way the holy people got power in the old days was through contact with the spirits of animals. Every winter they danced and danced. They just kept on dancing, and eventually they got very strong from the dancing and then power would come to them. But in those days everything was different. Clear air and many forests . . . So they could get in touch with the animals who gave them power. But I don't think they can do it anymore. Everything gone now—noise and all. Legend days are over. Civilization is coming. No more legend days. There will be no more.

Elizabeth Wilson (1881–1980)
Widow of Chief Joseph, Nez Percé

The historical perspective of *Legend Days* is based on early accounts of life on the Northern Plains, such as those found in George Bird Grinnell, J. W. Schultz, Walter McClintock, and the oral histories of the Blackfeet Confederacy. To all such sources, as well as the historical works of John C. Ewers and Beverly and Adolph Hungry Wolf, I offer my acknowledgements.

J. H.

Legend Days

One

I had to give up my life
in order to be.
GOETHE

It was in the winter that she changed into a man.

A breeze sprang up suddenly, coming down cold, damp, and with the odor of burning grass. She was a child, but she knew the sign very well. *Nat-ah-ki*, the Cold-Maker, was restless in his bed. Soon he would come howling down from the north, driving summer away and smothering the land in snow.

It was during the first storm that Amana changed. A strong man crept inside of her and refused to go away.

"Look at yourself," he whispered. "Your body does not know who you are."

And so he would not go away.

Amana struggled with him. At night she fought with him in her dreams. And in the daylight she tied him up and filled his mouth with ashes. But nothing she did or said would make him go away.

It was in that long-ago winter that Amana changed into a man.

Looking back, she saw the hills enveloped in a dense white fog. The daylight was swallowed by the vapor that tumbled down upon them. The sweat of the horses froze as they snorted and blew hard in the frigid air. The sky filled with fragments of silver frost that swirled upward in the wind.

"*Oo-ke!* . . . Let's go," her father shouted over the gale, hurrying his family toward the camp.

By the time Amana's family descended into the encampment of smoky tipis, the fog had changed into snow. There was good shelter in the deep valley of the river. The horses could feed upon the bark of the cottonwoods, and the lodges were protected by the brown thicket that had grown tall and green along the water's edge during the abundance of springtime. Now all the leaves had fallen from the branches, leaving glistening stems as the river turned to ice.

Amana and her family quickly set up their lodge. They were greeted by many noisy women who laughed and shouted as they came running through the whirlwind of snow, bringing glowing embers to light the cooking fire in Amana's lodge.

"*So-kah-pi* . . . Good," Amana's father sighed as he sat near the fire, smoking his pipe and watching his wife prepare the evening meal. "*Net-se-koo-nots* . . . I'm hungry," he

4

said, gazing at Amana and placing his wrinkled hand upon her head. "You are my silent baby-child," he murmured.

Amana shivered and opened her mouth without speaking.

"What is it that I see in your eyes, Amana?" he whispered as a look of terror came over the child's face.

Suddenly there was a scream from the sky. The tipi shook and twisted violently until all at once it tore open with a roar of thunder, and a huge white bird swooped down upon Amana's father, flapping its great jagged wings so powerfully that the fire scattered. Instantly the whole lodge ignited, and the flames leaped toward Amana.

"*E-spoom-mo-kin-on!* . . . Help us!" the old man shouted again and again as he thrashed his arms in the air, trying to drive the enormous bird from the flaming lodge.

People came running with water. Others began to shoot their rifles into the air, thinking the camp had been attacked. By the time they reached the tipi, it had burned to the ground, leaving all the possessions of the family buried in ashes.

"Ah . . ." they whimpered as they looked at the bewildered family. "Ah . . ." they whispered. A mysterious rush of wings silently swept between Amana's parents as they stood trembling in the wreckage.

"It was an owl!" the mother muttered, her face pale.

"Don't be afraid. We haven't done anything wrong," her husband said.

"It is a terrible sign!" his wife cried.

"Don't be afraid," he repeated as someone placed a buffalo robe over his shoulders.

"*Aih* . . . this is only the beginning," Amana's mother whimpered. "Something very bad is going to happen to you, my husband!" she exclaimed, drawing her robe over her head in fear.

"No," he insisted. "We have had enough misfortune. Our lodge is gone. It is snowing. The whole camp is frightened. And now we must beg shelter from our older daughter's husband. That is enough bad luck! No . . . nothing is going to happen to me."

It was in the winter of the white owl that Amana changed into a man.

A luminous ring encircled the weary moon. Everywhere in the darkness was the cry of birds. The night sky was filled with their invisible wings. And the people of the winter camp huddled close to their little fires and whispered about the terrible omens all around them.

In the yellow morning, sun dogs glowed through the snow-filled sky. The sun itself had vanished behind a mist of multicolored light.

No one ventured from the lodges. The children whispered. The women wept. But there were no morning songs.

Amana rubbed her small hands together fearfully as she crouched trembling in the lodge of her brother-in-law, Far

Away Son. She gazed in bewilderment as her tall, strong father hunched over the cold fire, panting silently. When he tried to go to his bed, he could not move. And when he tried to speak, no sound came from his throat. He sat motionless and silent except for his relentless panting. Just once during the terrible night, he had turned and stared at little Amana with such horror-filled eyes that she had cried out and hidden beneath her robe, whimpering until she fell asleep.

She was awakened by her mother's voice.

"He will not talk to me," she sobbed as Amana's married sister, SoodaWa, hurried back into the tipi with wood for the fire.

"I am here, Mama," SoodaWa said in a whisper as she coaxed the fire into dazzling flames. Then she embraced her mother and comforted her little sister. "Hush . . . hush, little one. Do not be afraid. I am here now. I am strong and I am not fearful of the omens. Everything is going to be all right now."

The mother moaned as she embraced her children and wept. "*Aih-o* . . . it is a bad day for all of us. During the summertime when we hunted alone, the land was good to us and the animals gave themselves to us. Now in this cold time, when we join our people in the winter camp, suddenly all the good days are gone. Our friends do not come to see us for fear of the omens. The camp is silent, and our relatives hide and will not comfort your father. *Aih-o* . . . what shall become of him? He does not lie down. He does not speak. He just sits by the fire and pants like a wounded animal!" Grasping her elder daughter's hand and pressing it tightly against her mouth, she groaned, "SoodaWa, I am afraid!"

SoodaWa gathered her wretched mother and Amana into her strong arms and rocked them gently. "Hush . . . hush," she murmured.

Gradually the sobs and whimpers subsided, and the three women sighed peacefully. SoodaWa gave her mother a bit of fat to eat, and she lifted Amana to her feet and wiped away her tears and brushed back her tangled black hair, gazing lovingly into the child's fearful eyes.

"And now," SoodaWa said softly, "we must be strong-hearted and gather our courage so we can help Mama and so we can comfort our father. Do you understand, Amana?"

Amana nodded.

"Good," SoodaWa said with a bright smile.

For a moment Amana gazed steadily at her elder sister, and gradually the fear vanished from her large eyes and she too smiled.

"Good," SoodaWa repeated happily as she hugged her mother and sent Amana to collect water.

When Amana returned to the lodge, the cooking fire was burning and sputtering, and her father was lying down and moaning very softly.

"Do you see," SoodaWa said with a tone of encouragement, "already he is feeling much better."

But it was not true—for the old man began to choke. He tossed violently, and a strange, rusty squawk came from his dry throat.

SoodaWa and her mother hurried to his bed and tried to quiet him. But the more they restrained him, the more he flapped his arms and croaked his strange cry.

"He wants water," SoodaWa exclaimed. "I'm sure of it! He needs water."

The mother quickly fetched water, and while her daughters stood anxiously by their father's side, she let one drop at a time drip into the old man's mouth. His eyes rolled and the rasp in his voice softened as he sank back into his bed.

"We must keep giving him water—day and night," SoodaWa said. "We can save him if we take turns watching over him. I'm sure of it."

And so, for two days, they stayed with the old man, and whenever he began to flap his arms and hoot and choke, they dripped water into his mouth. He swallowed it, little by little, and when he was content, he closed his eyes and fell back to sleep.

On the third day the two women were exhausted from their vigil, and the old man seemed so much improved that they went to bed, leaving Amana to watch over him.

Now there was not a sound in the lodge except the labored breathing of her father and the popping of the little fire. It was the hour of the morning star, and the wind was moving among the brittle branches of the thicket where the light was gradually making its way. The tracks of night animals rapidly filled with snow that came down in a vast, unbroken torrent. And for just a moment, Amana closed her eyes.

There was a sound.

She jumped to her feet and quickly fetched some water, for she was certain the croak that awakened her was her father's voice. But he was asleep.

"Ah . . ." whimpered Amana.

She crouched beside the old man in fear, and she began to tremble as she peered around and saw that the flap of the tipi was slowly opening.

In the doorway of the lodge stood a huge owl. He blinked his yellow eyes. He placed his large hands upon his groin and he smiled at Amana vaguely. "Come outside," he said. "I want you."

Amana screamed. Suddenly the fire lurched, throwing up a crimson flurry of sparks. When the smoke cleared, the owl had vanished, leaving only a glistening, red shadow hanging motionlessly in the doorway.

Amana was in her tenth winter when the owl spoke to her. And it was during that same winter that her father died.

Amana's mother fell over the body of her husband, and she bellowed a sorrowful song. She twisted and shuddered as she wept. Then she leaped to her feet and blindly searched for her husband's sharp flint knife; and she slashed her arms and legs, making the blood flow.

In the night she shouted at the moon as she hacked off her beautiful long black hair. She smeared her face with white clay, and she covered her body with rags and cinders. And then, when it was morning, she crawled back to the side of her dead husband with madness welling up in her eyes. She peered down at the pale face and lifeless limbs as the frenzy of her grief swelled into a long tormented howl. Her eyes and mouth remained wide open as she blindly snatched for her husband's knife. "*Aih-o!*" she shouted into the sky, throwing back her head and screaming. Then the knife came down hard and there was a silence as the scream dried up in her throat. She hung her head limply and gazed down at the blood-soaked ground. "*Aih-o. . . .*"

She had chopped off her little finger as a sacrifice to her dead husband.

Amana clung to her sister's side and watched fearfully as her mother limped from the camp and went to the top of the hill, where she threw herself down in the snow and wailed for the good man who would not return to her.

How empty this belly is
where you once made love!
What a meadow of sorrow
you have left for me!

Jamake Highwater

Now my breasts are blind,
and the dreams of a lifetime
have died with your thighs.

When the people of the winter camp heard the lamentation, they hurried to the place where the dead man had kept his horses, and they took all but the oldest of them. The women scratched through the debris of the widow's lodge and took everything of value. This was the custom; this was the way a dead man's life was thrown to the wind.

SoodaWa was a strong woman with a courageous heart, but she would do nothing to prevent the raid upon her father's property. A man owned nothing but his own body, and the rest of his possessions were returned to the tribe when he died, just as he returned to the sky and the earth and the rivers.

When SoodaWa's old husband, Far Away Son, came back to camp and saw what the people were doing, he realized at once that his father-in-law was dead. He dropped the meat he had brought from the hunt and he covered his head in sorrow. Feeble women who had waited for the younger people to claim plunder were still snatching at the last few belongings of the dead man when Far Away Son entered the death lodge. He made no effort to stop them. It would have been unworthy of the memory of the dead to notice what was happening in the lodge. And so, glancing away with tears in his eyes, he sank to the ground and slowly murmured a prayer.

The next morning the women of the camp dressed the corpse in fine clothing, and they sewed the body into a buffalo robe—the only possessions that had been left for the burial. Carefully, they laid the dead man upon a platform of poles in the center of his lodge and stood silently while the wind rippled through the vacant lodge.

SoodaWa and Far Away Son selected the best horse left in the herd and covered its flanks with vivid images of the dead man's courageous deeds. They painted with tears in their eyes, and they sang a forlorn song as they braided the horse's chestnut mane and tail and placed an elegant saddle hide on its broad back. Then, while Amana stumbled along in the deep snow, stunned by the solemnity of the procession, the people of the winter camp carried the body to a tall tree, where they lashed it in the fork of the highest branches.

Amana watched in silence. She could hear nothing but the dirge of the wind, echoing over the silent, snowy landscape, twisting like a song in the pine trees and among the leafless dogwoods. SoodaWa slowly led the painted horse to the tree, glancing upward toward the bundled body of her father. Then Far Away Son stepped forward and took the reins. The animal nervously shifted its weight as it blew hard in the icy air.

Tears filled Amana's eyes. She looked away as Far Away Son pressed his rifle to the horse's chestnut head.

The crack of the explosion rebounded across the valley.

The animal shuddered. Suddenly blood gushed from its

13

flared nostrils. Then its delicate legs buckled. The massive body crashed to the ground, where its blood slowly turned the snow crimson.

The carcass was left where it had fallen, and the people of the camp silently returned to their lodges. Their footprints filled quickly with new snow. The wind hovered over the death tree. And silence turned the red heap of the horse's body into a frozen tomb.

Soon the wolves picked up the scent and cautiously circled the dead animal. When it was night, their howls resounded across the valley, and the people made large fires to comfort their children.

That same night the widow was carried to the lodge of Far Away Son. Like her husband, she could not move or speak. Friends who had come to give condolences withdrew in dread. They covered their faces when they saw the woman sweating upon her couch. They whispered among themselves in fear.

"It is the sickness!" they gasped.

"Look how she vomits blood!"

"It is the sickness!"

"I have seen this before," an old woman moaned as she fearfully hugged her grandchildren. "In the time of Calf Chief, the sickness killed almost all of our people! I tell you," she cried, "I know this sickness! It has come back for those of us who escaped it!"

For two days the widow lay upon her couch, sweating

14

and shivering with fever. She groaned with pain in her head and back, and she vomited until her body shook with convulsions. When SoodaWa pulled back the robe to bathe her mother, she discovered that a rash covered her stomach and thighs. By the third day sores began to appear on the woman's forehead. They spread rapidly and itched so intensely that SoodaWa had to tie down her mother's hands to prevent her from tearing at her flesh. Soon the widow's body was covered with large boils. They swelled until they turned yellow and burst. The fluid oozed over the body, and the skin became rancid and stank so vilely that her children became ill as they approached her.

SoodaWa and Far Away Son constantly tended the stricken woman. When one of them slept, the other hovered over the agonized body and applied cold water to the massive lacerations. Amana crept to her mother's side. She gazed down into the familiar face, but it was so disfigured by running cankers that the child could not recognize it. Her mother tried to speak as her swollen eyes stared up in horror through corruption and pus. The voice was so hoarse Amana could not understand her mother's frantic whispers.

"Come away!" SoodaWa screeched as she grabbed her little sister and lifted her into her arms. "Don't look anymore, Amana! Don't look!" she wailed. "Go out . . . go outside before the sickness catches you! Do you hear me? Get out quickly!" And she pushed Amana into the night and would not let her back into the lodge. "Run!" she shouted as she drove her sister into the darkness. "Run and hide and do not come back until all of us are dead!"

Amana began to cry as she stumbled through the snow. She began to scream as she rushed between the dark lodges where she could hear the moaning of all the people dying of the sickness.

KAAAAAAAAAAAAAH!

Suddenly the branches of the trees burst open and there was a frantic flapping of wings. Amana threw open her arms and clutched at the ground as great claws grasped her shoulders. She howled and kicked and fought as she was swept high into the air.

When finally she landed and opened her eyes, she found herself in the immense lodge of the owls, piled with the bones of rabbits and mice. The owl that had carried her off giggled when she cried, and he gruffly pushed her into the center of the lodge.

"Grandfather," he called to the old owl-man slouched near the fire, "look what I have brought you!"

"What is it?" the old owl muttered. "What good is it?"

"It's something nice for you to have."

"Good," the grandfather said, gazing at Amana's arms and legs and rubbing his white feathers together gleefully. "Leave it here and go away."

The young owl hesitated.

"Did you hear me? Leave it . . . just leave it and go away!"

Reluctantly the young bird backed out of the lodge, leaving Amana alone with grandfather owl.

He continued to peer at her silently for a long time. Then he stood up and closed his elegant feathered robe around his shoulders and hobbled on his skinny old legs in a circle around Amana.

"Good," he said. "You can sleep over there in the corner," he told her, pointing to the women's place in the lodge. "And when it is morning you can get busy and try to make yourself useful."

Amana crept into the corner and curled up on the bare ground. Then, when the grandfather returned to his place by the fire, she began to weep.

"What is the matter with you, child?" the old owl demanded.

"I want to go home," Amana murmured.

The grandfather laughed. "This is your home. Go to sleep."

But Amana could not sleep. She remembered the swollen eyes of her mother, and her sister's terrified voice. And she could not sleep. All night there was the sound of beating wings as the owls swept into the air, as they swooped down on rabbits and mice, and dragged the broken little bodies to their lodges high in the trees.

All around Amana the owls chuckled and squawked as they plunged their beaks into the squirming creatures and tore away their flesh. By the time it was morning, they had

17

finished their meal and nothing remained but heaps of delicate little bones.

"Wake up!" grandfather owl exclaimed as he shook Amana. "I can't stand the light of the sun. Do you understand me? So you will have to do all the work in the daytime. Do you hear me, child?" he demanded, continuing to shake Amana. "If you don't work, you won't get anything to eat!"

Amana scrambled to her feet and gazed at the old owl.

"Don't be afraid," he said. "No one will harm you if you do what you are told. Go outside and get wood for the fire."

Amana hurried from the lodge and climbed down to the ground. As she shivered in the cold, picking up branches and sticks, a fox emerged from the trunk of a dead tree. The creature was very large and beautiful. Her breasts were supple and her belly was filled with unborn children. For a long time she stood looking at Amana. Then she brushed back her long red fur and shook her head in pity.

"You do not know it, child," she said softly, "but you are gathering that firewood for yourself. They are going to cook you, child. They are going to eat you!"

"No," exclaimed Amana, "you are wrong. The grandfather promised that he would not hurt me!"

Then, without speaking again, the fox laughed and disappeared into the tree stump.

Frightened, Amana ran back to the owl's lodge.

"That's not enough wood," the grandfather grunted impatiently. "I told you to get firewood, not a few twigs! Get out of here and don't come back until you bring a big armful of wood!"

Amana hurried out once again and quickly hunted all the large branches she could find and carried them back to the lodge. But the grandfather was still unsatisfied.

"Not enough! Not nearly enough! How can I cook my dinner with that little pile of wood? You'll never make a good wife!" the owl shouted. "What man wants a woman who can't find enough firewood to cook dinner!"

Amana began to weep as she ran out of the lodge once again and frantically searched for more wood.

As she was collecting sticks and digging in the snow for fallen branches, the fox reappeared and gazed at her.

"You must be careful," the fox whispered. "I have tried to warn you. The fire you are building will be the fire in which you burn. You must listen to me and you must not go back to the owls!"

"But what shall I do? And where can I go?"

The fox leaped to the ground and took the wood from Amana's hands. "Quickly," she murmured, "get on my back. I will take you to a safe place and I will tell you what you must do." As soon as Amana had leaped on the fox and grabbed her shoulders, they dashed headlong into the forest, across the frozen lakes and up to the top of a great mountain.

They stopped in front of a large, jagged rock at the summit, and they sat in the snow while the fox explained to Amana that she must speak to the rock. "Now do exactly what I have told you," the fox demanded.

Amana stood up slowly. She was weak, for she had not slept or eaten. But she summoned all her courage as she faced the rock towering before her. Then she spoke.

"Grandfather! Listen to me! I have come to you for protection. Father! Listen to me! I have come to you for protection. Brother! I have come here for your protection. Husband! I have come this long way for your protection!"

There was a growl in the earth, and then the rock slowly rolled aside. Behind it was a large cave where a magnificent red fox sat upon many rich furs.

"Come to me, child," he said. "You will be safe here."

Amana crept into the cave. As soon as she was inside, the rock rolled back and blocked the entrance.

At last Amana felt safe. The sickness could not get her, and the owls could not find her. Without speaking another word, she lay down among the fox furs and fell asleep at once.

Before long, however, the earth shook, and from the distance came the sound of hooting.

"It is grandfather owl," the old fox whispered, covering Amana with his robe and comforting her. "He is looking for you, child."

Amana sat up in dread. Four times the owl hooted, and four times the earth shook. The last time the owl hooted,

he was just beyond the great rock that sealed the cave of grandfather fox.

She could hear the owl snapping and snarling as he flapped his wings and sniffed the ground for Amana.

"Give me back my meat!" he hooted angrily. "Bring that child out here or I'll come in and get her!"

Amana begged grandfather fox to help her.

"Do exactly as I say," the old fox whispered. "Put your hands on the rock that blocks the door and roll it away just enough for the owl to get his head inside the cave."

Amana crept to the entrance, and with all her power she pressed against the great rock. At first it would not budge, but then gradually it began to roll back. When the rock moved aside, the owl instantly thrust in his head and opened wide his terrible beak. Amana yelled with fear and leaped out of his reach. Then suddenly the rock thundered back into place, cutting off grandfather owl's head.

When the dismembered body of the owl had been skinned and burned in the fire, grandfather fox smiled at Amana. He gave her berries to eat. And he blessed her with the blessing of the foxes. And then he withdrew into the darkness.

Once again Amana curled up among the soft furs on the cave floor and happily went to sleep.

She dreamed of the eyes of the fox. And she dreamed of the songs and dances that gave the foxes their power. While she slept and dreamed, many seasons passed. The snow disappeared from the sky, and then the warm wind came

down into the valley. The earth began to awaken, and the great rock, ripened by the sun, rolled away from the entrance and allowed the daylight to stream into the cave of the foxes.

When Amana felt the warmth of her eleventh springtime upon her newmade body, she slowly opened her eyes. She was astonished, for she was no longer a child. During her long, long dream, something marvelous had happened to her body. Like the springtime berries, she felt ripe and whole. Like the little rivers, her blood flowed rich and warm from its winter's sleep. Excitedly, Amana searched for grandfather fox, but he had vanished. All the foxes were gone. But in their place was a trove of magical things. There was a crimson robe and a pair of handsome moccasins and glorious leggings like those worn by the most favored sons. There was also a thunder bow with bright lightning painted upon its sturdy back, and the skin of a prairie owl, and a drum that knew all the sacred songs of the kit foxes. All these powerful things had been left for Amana when she awakened from her childhood.

Amana drew the breath of life into her chest. The great white gust of air filled her with the power of the fox. And in that sudden wind came a song that spoke to her.

"I am your dream," it said. "I am the seed that grows. I am the cave of your heart and the drum that summons legends and dreams. Listen to me and listen to me well, for I will not sing this song again in all your days. It is a

22

whisper in your ear. It is the drumming of your spirit. And it can be heard by no one but you, Amana—for its power lives in silence. You may not speak of it. You may not boast of it. You may not wear your hero's clothes for others to see. These gifts we give to you are the gifts of silence. Their strength will vanish and the dream will die if you speak of them. Only once may you come to your people in your splendid regalia—so those of wisdom will recognize the promise of your power. And then you must take this vision we give to you and draw it into your heart, where it must remain like the storm that fills the cloud with lightning. Listen to me and listen well, for I will not sing again!"

Amana outfitted herself in the splendid regalia of a warrior, and following the instructions of the voice that spoke within her, she painted her face red and tied the skin of grandfather owl upon her forehead. She sang the song of the fox and she pranced lightly on her feet to the steps of the fox-power dance. And when she was finally dressed, she was utterly transformed. She came out of the cave more handsome and strong than the greatest of young warriors. And the voice within her said: "I am the man within you, Amana. You must keep me hidden or I will lose my power. You must honor me or you will foresake your vision. I am the vision that gives you great strength. I am your warrior; I am your spirit guide. Listen to me and you will prosper. But you must keep me hidden. You must nourish me and honor me, but you may wear my regalia only when you are alone. These things you must do, or I shall abandon you to the owls, and all your strength will vanish, and all your visions will dissolve, and nothing will remain for you but the world of daylight."

And thus it happened in the time of the white owl and the kit fox that Amana changed into a man.

And coming out of the cave of the foxes, dressed in the regalia of the warrior who lived within her, Amana searched the horizon for the valley where long ago, when she had been a child, she had been sent away by her sister SoodaWa and she had fled from the great sickness.

There was no sound as Amana approached the camp. A horrible stench permeated the air. When she came to the first tipi, she saw the grim remains of her people. Countless skeletons were scattered everywhere among the ruins of the lodges. There seemed to be no survivors. The sickness had killed SoodaWa, Far Away Son . . . everyone.

Amana's tears flowed into the warrior's eyes, though he fought them back valiantly. Then, when he was about to turn away from the desolation of the camp of many seasons past, a sound, a feeble little sound, broke the stillness. "Ah!" Amana rejoiced. "Someone is still alive!"

By the river two old women were lying helplessly on the ground. One of them was blind and the other was crippled.

"Dead . . ." they mumbled again and again. "All of them dead."

Then one of them gazed up at Amana and began to weep. "You are a strong young man," she pleaded, trying to stand on her feeble legs. "You must put an end to this misery! Kill us, my grandson; kill us quickly so we can lie down with our grandchildren!"

Amana embraced the old women and gave them food and water. She carried them to the shade, and after she had buried their grandchildren under a mound of rocks, she peered around the desolate encampment.

"Has no one survived? Is there no one else?" she murmured.

"Dead . . ." the old women intoned dolefully.

"Is no one left of my family? Are they all gone?" Amana whispered.

"Who are you?" one of the women asked, staring into Amana's face, trying to recognize the handsome young man. "What tribe are you? Where have you come from?"

Suddenly Amana began to weep. She embraced the grandmothers of her people and fell to the ground and shook with sobs. "I am Amana," she sighed. "I am the child called Amana, and my sister is called SoodaWa. A great vision has filled me with its power. It has placed a dream within my heart, and that dream is full of the legends of my days."

"*Aih!*" exclaimed one of the old women as she gazed in wonder at Amana. "It was that power that kept you alive!

And in your eyes I see the power of your vision. This dream will make you strong. It will give you wisdom and courage. I can see it in your face, and I can hear its loud singing in your hero's heart. And yet I also see the pain and torment this great vision will bring to you—for it is said that to be unlike the world is to be alone in a world of your own. Even the wisest of our people will be blind to your vision, Amana. And the summers of your life will be like the deepest winters when the trees are leafless and the days are difficult and lean. *Aih,*" the old woman counseled, "there are dark times ahead of you, and you must be prepared for them or you will be crushed. There is great trouble, and there is also great power in your dream. You must keep your dream alive, Amana—or the bad days will tumble over you like an avalanche. And our people shall be destroyed!"

"These things I have promised to keep alive in the silence within me. And I will protect the dream so it will grow," Amana whispered to the old women.

"*Aih!*" they murmured reverently. "You will be one of the great ones, child. Yes, it is true. You are one of the women whose name will be remembered."

The old women wept joyously. One of them, who could not see, nodded as she touched the ground with her fingertips, while the other woman gazed into Amana's eyes until she was certain that she was truly the little girl they had known before the sickness had come. And when they recognized her they began to weep in thanksgiving.

"I am Crow Woman," said one of the elders. "And my sister, who cannot see with her eyes but has great vision of the mind, is called Weasel Woman. And you! Look at you! Some very great power has protected you, Amana. Some spirit has changed you into a man and has given you your life!"

"Yes, I am alive . . . but did none of the rest of my family survive?" Amana asked softly.

"Some . . . some may yet live. When the dying began there was great confusion. The young men killed themselves rather than allow the sickness to turn them into monstrosities. Women threw their babies into the river when they began to scream with the agony of the cankers.

"One of the first to die was Chief Seen From Afar. Then all the others began to perish. The babies screamed night and day. The children died first and then the men. The women dragged the living out of the lodges and tried to move the camp to higher ground. But the horses fell into the snow and would not move. And the dogs had gone mad with hunger and soon they began to attack anyone who was too weak to fight them off or shoot them.

"My son died while I tried to drag him to the river," Crow Woman wailed as she swayed to and fro and wept. "I tried to drive away the sickness, but it was too strong. My songs were of no use to me. Nothing could help him.

"It came from the river. They say the sickness came from the boat that makes smoke on the river. The white men on the river brought it with them in their boat, just as they did when I was a child. It is the white men who brought the sickness."

"And SoodaWa?" Amana asked. "Do you know what became of my sister, SoodaWa?"

The old women nodded their heads listlessly, gazing off blankly. Then Weasel Woman sighed and said, "On the night that your mother died . . . on that same night your sister and her husband tried to leave the camp."

"SoodaWa came to me," Crow Woman recalled, "because all of your father's horses had been stolen or had died. She begged me for one of our horses so she and Far Away Son could escape. I gave her the horse. I gave her whatever she wanted. Already my husband was dead and my son was dying. So I gave her whatever she wanted. I told her to take anything. But when I looked at her, I could see the sores on her forehead, and I knew that she already had the sickness and could not escape."

Amana covered her face and sighed with dread and sorrow.

"Far Away Son and your sister left the camp at night. It was snowing hard, and they had only one horse for the two of them. I remember Far Away Son had to lash your sister to his body to keep her from falling off the horse . . . she was so sick she could not stay awake.

"And then," Crow Woman whispered, pointing to the mountains, "they disappeared."

The man inside of Amana sat down on the ground and wept. And after he had wept, he took off the marvelous clothing of the warrior—the crimson robe, the moccasins, the leggings, the thunder bow, the skin of the owl—and he wrapped them carefully into a bundle. He wrapped the drum that knew the songs of the foxes. And all of these holy things he hid away as he had been instructed to do.

The old women gave him bits of their ragged clothing, and he dressed slowly as he silently sang a sacred song in his heart. And when he had finished, he was Amana once again.

"We alone know the great power you received from the foxes," Crow Woman mumured. "But we shall tell no one. That is our promise to you, Amana, for you have saved us. We are faithful women who have twice made vows to the Sun. We are old and useless, but we are filled with love for you. I cannot walk well and my sister cannot see. But we will be your grandmothers, and we will love you and keep your secret well, Amana."

Gathering a few possessions from the camp of the dead, they laboriously traveled to a high mountain valley, a vast meadow of long bunch grass and yellow wild flowers, surrounded by a dense forest of pine, fir, and spruce. There they set up two lodges. They made a good fire, and they prayed for food and safety.

There were many animals in the valley—whitetail and blacktail deer, elk, moose, grizzly bear, and wolverine. But what good were such fine game to two old women and a girl?

"We have a rifle and we have a bow, but these are not

things that women are taught to use," Crow Woman complained. "We can do many important things, but we do not know how to hunt."

Then the old woman cunningly gazed at Amana, hoping she might open her sacred bundle and put on the clothes of the warrior and hunt for them. But Amana turned away and climbed to the summit of the mountain above the camp, saying to herself, "It is forbidden. It is my oath to keep the warrior within me hidden until the song of the fox comes into my heart."

Alone at the summit of the mountain, she searched in every direction for some sign of her people. But the land was silent and motionless. No smoke. No fires. No dust from horses and travois. No sign of her people anywhere. Every evening Amana climbed to the summit and peered off into the great expanse of the land. But there was never a sign of a living person.

There was little to eat. Grandma Crow Woman tried to snare grouse and prairie chickens, but they were too fast for her. In desperation, she hobbled along, following the mouse trails in the grass to find their little nests so she could raid them for the lily roots the mice gathered. She stumbled along on her weak, skinny legs, following the little marks left by the mice as they hurried through the grass. She had to sit down very often to rest, and she complained about the pain in her hip. But eventually she discovered a mouse nest and shouted so joyously that her voice resounded through the little mountain valley and her blind sister, Weasel Woman, momentarily put aside the moccasins she was sewing and joined in the victory whoop.

Crow Woman also showed Amana how to hunt for bird nests. In the morning they would go out together to the creek that flowed through the valley, and Amana would fill the water vessels while Grandmother Crow Woman sniffed the air and walked in wide circles in the flowering meadow, hunting for egg-laden nests.

But soon even this miserable supply of food was exhausted. Weasel Woman lay on her couch and whimpered quietly while her sister stirred grass and grubs into a wretched stew. Amana grew weak and thin. Finally, one morning, Crow Woman could not get up from her bed. She cried out: "Have pity on us, Sun," when the morning sky turned brilliant with the approach of day. "Take pity on this child you have given to us, Sun. Do not allow those who survived the sickness to die now of hunger!"

The old women choked and sighed when Amana tried to give them water. They would not look at her and they waved her away. "Leave us now, child, leave us," they groaned. "For we must sing our death songs."

Amana begged Crow Woman to try to get up, but she refused. She lay silently on her couch and closed her eyes.

"Please do not die!" Amana pleaded.

But the old women only wept as they lay helplessly upon their beds.

Confused and frightened, Amana staggered to the summit over the valley, and once again she searched in every direction for some sign of help. There was no one.

She shouted into the vast landscape that surrounded her. Still there was no reply.

Then, as she sank to the ground and gazed aimlessly into her hands, the sacred song of the foxes came into her heart, faintly at first and then louder and louder until it filled her entire body. Amana opened her mouth and threw back her head as she let the song pour from her throat. And as she sang an immense power filled her.

She hurried back to the lodges, where she took the sacred bundle from its special place. She laid it upon a fur robe between the old women, who now lay pale and silent, and with the smoke of sweet grass she anointed the bundle. Then she unwrapped the drum, and it sprang up and began to sing a powerful song. Amana carefully unwrapped the bundle containing the clothing of a warrior. She quickly dressed in the splendid regalia. Then she took Crow Woman's rifle and hurried away toward the forest.

She did not understand the power that filled her. She did not know where it came from. Yet her hands knew the rifle and knew exactly how to hold it. She was bewildered, but at the same time she was wild with courage. As she rushed through the low-hanging branches, something guided her feet and eyes. When she came to a clearing, she searched the ground for signs. There—just in front of her—were the heavy tracks of a fearsome grizzly bear. Instead of being frightened, she was excited. It was a dream that appeared suddenly and changed everything it touched. It was like the images found in the fingertips of those who painted the robes and the tipis. It was like the power that put a new song in the mouth of the singer.

"Ah!" Amana exclaimed, raising her rifle into the air. "Who speaks to me with my own voice?"

She whirled around and saw a huge doe shaking its head, snorting, and stretching its long neck as she rushed toward her. Amana took careful aim. The rifle roared. And then, as she lowered her weapon, tears came into her eyes. The animal crashed to the ground, kicking its delicate legs among the flowers. And then it lay very still as a rich stream pulsated slowly from its shattered head.

Grandmother Crow Woman groaned as she feebly pried open the deer's skull and scooped out its brains. Weasel Woman made a feast of the raw liver and nose gristle, while Amana ate the dark-red organs, the kidneys, relished by men. When they had finally satisfied their overwhelming hunger, they sighed and contentedly fell asleep where they lay. By the morning their strength had returned, and they set to work properly butchering every part of the animal that had given them its life so they might live. Crow Woman cleaned sections of the small intestine, turning the fat inside,

33

and Weasel Woman (moving her blind eyes to and fro as her hands worked from memory) cut long, thin strips of the meat and stuffed them into the intestine, which was then cooked over the fire on a wooden spit. Amana hacked the ribs of the beast into large segments and roasted them on a bed of coals. And for dessert Crow Woman prepared a favorite soup made from the mixture of deer fat, berries, and blood. The aroma of the feast was marvelous. The scented smoke rose and blanketed the meadow. Amana began to sing as the dinner cooked, and her grandmothers joined in the song of victory. They thanked the earth for its beauty and they sang in homage of the doe who had given her life to them.

Then the women set to work on the large carcass, cutting the meat that was left into long, narrow pieces which they hung up on branches to dry in the sun. And when it was finally evening and their task was completed at last, each of them went silently to the edge of the forest and, climbing high into a spruce, left a morsel of meat tied to a branch in gratitude for their survival and good fortune.

Now the cooking fire flickered softly in the night. The mockingbirds began their evening songs. Amana gazed lovingly at the regalia that grandfather fox had given her, and then, a bit sadly, she returned the clothing of the warrior to its bundle and dressed once again as a woman.

"For this power you have given me in your song, for this knowledge you have given me as a hunter, and because you allowed me to call upon my secret so I could save my grandmothers, for all of these things I thank you, grandfather fox. And I will keep my oath and I will keep you hidden from the eyes of strangers. All these things I promise," Amana chanted quietly from the summit of the mountain. And then she returned to the camp. And after the women had embraced one another, they went to sleep, feeling happy and full for the first time in many nights.

The summer sun quickly dried the meat. The grandmothers busied themselves packing it in rawhide bundles, separating the layers of dried meat with layers of uncooked back fat, wild peppermint, and sarvis berries. In the daytime Amana crept through the forest in search of small game, and in the evenings she and the two old women chanted and prayed. But during all these happy days of summer they had seen no one in the meadow. The land was filled with sounds, but there were no human voices. Amana's shouts from the mountaintop went unanswered day after day, and the fire that Grandmother Weasel Woman kept burning had attracted no one. It seemed to them that the sickness had killed everybody in the world. And Crow Woman wept at the thought of it. And Weasel Woman murmured, "Soon it will be the time of the Sun Dance, and there will be no holy ones to celebrate it."

But there was little time for complaint. Winter was coming, and the women knew they would be all alone to face the Cold-Maker.

The grandmothers worked until they were exhausted. They made pemmican, cooking and pounding dried meat and mixing it with boiled marrow grease. With a stone hammer Weasel Woman mashed the pits and pulp of dried chokecherries and added the sweet paste to the pemmican, which she carefully stored in bags she had sewn from the skins of rabbits. Amana used every hunting skill she had learned from the fox, but as the days grew short, the animals began to leave the meadow and fresh meat became scarce.

"Soon it will be time for us to leave the meadow too," Grandmother Crow Woman told them.

"We have worked hard but we still do not have enough for the winter," Weasel Woman said as her fingers rapidly worked the binding of the moccasins she was making.

The evenings grew cool, and Amana collected a large stack of wood which Weasel Woman piled upon the fire until it filled the lodge with warmth. The night murmured with the sigh of the meadow grass, which had already turned dry and golden. The wild flowers were gone. The cones dropped from the pines in the deep silence of the forest. The cottonwoods were brilliant yellow and orange. And in the sky unbroken flocks of birds streamed southward like a leaf-filled wind.

One afternoon Crow Woman went into the meadow and collected the gray-colored plant called women's sage, and then she and Weasel Woman twined the leaves into small pads and blessed them with the smoke of the long grass. Amana examined these pads and was perplexed. Her grand-mothers smiled.

"You are no longer a girl," Crow Woman explained when the evening meal ended and they sat huddled around the fire. "Now a great river begins to flow within you, Amana. It is a powerful stream which comes, like the water of the mountain springs, from the great mystery that made the stars and all that lives upon the earth. And that is what these pads made from women's sage are for, Amana. Do you understand?"

"*Aih!*" Amana exclaimed with annoyance. "I don't want to be a woman! Grandfather fox promised that I would live with a great warrior within me! That was his promise!"

"Yes, yes, we know, Amana," Weasel Woman said patiently. "You had a great vision and you have already received much power. This summer you have become a hunter. But you must also be a woman who knows the duties of the lodge. You are both warrior and woman. That is how it is with you, Amana. That is what your vision in the cave of the foxes has taught you. And you must accept what has been given to you."

"But I don't want to be a woman!" Amana repeated with tears coming into her eyes.

"Suffering brings vision to those who know how to see through their pain," Crow Woman whispered, comforting

Amana with an embrace. "Your mother and father would be very proud of you. They would make many offerings of thanksgiving for the vision that was given to you by the great mystery. But they would also tell you what I now tell you, Amana: You must keep the warrior hidden within you, and you must become a good woman."

"I will not do it!" Amana wept bitterly. "I want to sing my strong song! I want to hunt! I want to dress in my beautiful leggings and moccasins! I don't want anything to do with your ugly women's sage!"

"We are your grandmothers now," Weasel Woman insisted as she took Amana by the shoulders. "It is our duty to teach you all that we know, and it is your duty to listen to us. In the days ahead you must come to understand not only your powers as a man but also your powers as a woman. The flow that will soon begin in your body is strong. It is the miracle of being a woman!"

"This winter," Crow Woman added in a strong voice, "is the most important time of your life, for everything you do will mark you for all your days. A girl who does not work hard during the winter of her first flow will turn out to be a lazy wife. That is what our mothers taught us, and that is what our mother's mothers taught them. If you eat too much you will become fat and greedy. If you talk too much, you will become a gossip; and if you lie, then you will be dishonest forever. These are the days in which you become a woman, Amana, and they are like the first season of a tree—wherever it plants its roots, there shall it grow."

38

"You know from your mother and your grandmothers all the stories of Napi—the Old Man who made the world and everything in it," Weasel Woman continued in a soft, chanting voice, reaching deep within herself to find the tales of her people. "You know that to each and every possible thing Old Man gave a good place. You know that he hates nothing, but loves everything and everyone that exists. And so it is now—there can be nothing in the world of Napi that does not have its place and its purpose. All this you know. . . ."

"And so it is," Crow Woman continued where Weasel Woman left off, "you have been given this special vision of yourself that is not quite the same as the way any other person has ever known herself before. It is a strange thing that you have become. We understand this vision no better than you understand it, Amana. But we know that in the world of Napi anything is possible. In the world of Napi, you may be both a man and a woman, each in its own time. This is the gift that you have been given, Amana. And you will accept that gift and you will learn to be happy with it. That is the lesson of this winter of your first flow, Amana."

"Do you understand what we have been telling you?" Weasel Woman asked with a gentle gesture of her head.

For a very long time Amana did not respond. She gazed at her hands and sighed. Then at last she looked into the faces of her grandmothers, and an expression of determination came into her eyes.

The grandmothers smiled warmly and embraced Amana.

"Good!" they laughed merrily. And then they sang a song of the power of women, raising their voices very high to the loftiest notes of the birds.

Amana closed her eyes, feeling deep within her body the power of the great mystery. She too began to sing, first with the deep tones of the warrior and then, gradually, with the thin, bright, cascading tones of the women. The song flew into the air like an arrow, turning first into green leaves and then into the soft tender bodies of new-made things. The song grew in its strength and the song grew in its power until at last the night was filled with its immense beating heart, filling the women with life and drumming deep within their memories where the faces of their mothers and their mothers' mothers smiled and wept and groaned in labor.

It was a night of many flying stars and there was much wind among the cottonwoods. The voices of the night rose with the song of the women. And everything was slowly turning in the air.

They spoke of children and of cooking and of sewing. And they whispered about the plants that are used by brides. They talked about the warm bodies of men and the enormous ringing pleasure of their love. They murmured about the silent peace and passivity of the dreams that filled their sleeping. And about solitude and about the strength of a woman's mind and body. They explained the moons of waiting, when the child grows within a woman's belly, and of its urgent nudging to be born. And they spoke of the old women who made images of snakes and butterflies and gave them to women who did not wish to have children. And they also spoke of the images of animals favored by women who longed for infants. And then they sent their song high into the air where the stars burst into their separate fires in celebration of the mystery of creation and of the place in the solitary stone where the mountain begins.

Crow Woman shook with happiness as she hugged Amana. "And so you understand," she said, "how very special it is to be a woman."

"Yes," Amana agreed with some reluctance as she gazed at the bundle in which her warrior's regalia was hidden. "But I would rather be a woman all by myself than be a woman with a man."

The grandmothers laughed and shook their heads with amused impatience. "*Aih*, my child, you are surely the most stubborn of all Napi's people. But believe me, one day— one lovely, sunlit day, you will change your mind at least for a little while. You will meet a man, and even that stubborn warrior within you will learn to love him. Yes, Amana, you will see—you will love him until your heart makes you dizzy with the fragrance of him, with his arms and his eyes and his hair. And then, for a little while you will not be a warrior. You will put aside your weapons against love and you will cease to resist the woman within you. And then, my child, you will realize both the power and the powerlessness of being a woman."

By autumn their travois was loaded with pemmican, and the time had come for them to follow the animals north and to pick a good camping place where they might find protection from the howling blizzards and snows of winter. The sun glowed orange and golden in the midafternoon as shadows crossed the silent grasses, bringing night earlier and earlier each day. It was a sad time for the women, for now they faced a long and lonely winter of solitude. It was also a sad time for Amana. For as many seasons as she could recall, her tribe had always assembled into a vast winter encampment. All the small bands that spent the summer alone in their far-flung hunting grounds joined together in a glistening community of tipis, sending up smoke and the sounds of laughter and winter games. How nice it used to be when all the people gathered together in the time of the Cold-Maker.

"*Aih*," Grandmother Weasel Woman exclaimed as she embraced Amana with an expression of sorrow in her face, "but we are alone now. All the people were taken by the sickness and we are alone. So we must fend for ourselves through the hard wintertime."

They broke camp before sunrise, and in a cool breeze that pressed hard upon them from the mountains, they started on their way. Amana and blind Weasel Woman pulled the heavy travois while Crow Woman, with the aid of a cottonwood cane, stumbled along after them, singing into the wind.

They left the shelter of their handsome valley in the mountains and followed a shady forest trail that wound through the rusty-brown foothills. Already the first frosts had turned the grasses umber and dry. Then they descended over high ridges and turned northward along the prairies that spread out beneath the giant peaks. The crickets sang and on every side were the broad meadows and rolling swells of brown grasslands. The small lakes were filled with noisy flocks of ducks and geese pausing on their southward migrations.

On their journey the women followed the Old North Trail, the most traveled of all the ancient routes of the Northwest. It ran along the great chain of mountains called the Backbone of the World, winding over the smooth, rounded ridges and then down long slopes, through wide meadows, and across blue streams and gray rivers, clear and icy cold.

At the head of a broad and windy valley they saw the peak of Chief Mountain, a lone spur of rock, a huge wall rising into the clouds above the surrounding plain.

The women were exhausted from their long, hard journey. Each day they pressed forward, and at night they made camp in groves of shaking aspen, among big cottonwoods in river valleys, and on the banks of swift-flowing streams. But during all these difficult days they saw no one. They found no tracks of other travelers. And they could hear no trace of human voices in the wind that brought the smallest and most distant sound across the great plains.

Then one evening, when they were searching for a camping place, Amana thought she heard an unfamiliar noise. It came from very far away and was very faint, but she was certain that it was a dog or a horse or perhaps a person. Without saying a word she dropped her burden and ran ahead of the old women, peering into the darkening landscape. In the distance, where the endless plains reached the sky, she thought for a moment that she saw a whiff of smoke. But she was not certain. It could have been just a cloud or a dust devil.

"What do you see? What is it?" the grandmothers exclaimed as they rushed to where Amana was standing.

She silenced them with a gesture and did not speak, for fear of losing sight of the apparition in the distance.

There was another sound. "It is!" Amana shouted. "It is a dog! I tell you . . . there are people out there!"

The women resumed their difficult journey, dragging their possessions as quickly as they could and never taking their eyes from the spectre of color that marked the otherwise desolate plain.

It was not until deep night covered the land in darkness that they were certain of what they had urgently hoped:

There truly were people camped far out on the flatlands. As the sky dimmed and the moon hid behind a thick overcast, they made out the remote little flash of a campfire— like a star in the deepest, darkest heaven, beckoning to them.

The old women shouted with delight, but they did not hesitate for a moment in their slow progress across the plains.

In the days before the sickness there had been so many enemy tribes crossing the plains that it was not safe to travel by daylight. The grandmothers had often crossed this same wide region at night in the days when there were many war parties prowling the tall, dry grass in search of the chattels of unwary travelers. But tonight they were not afraid. Even if the encampment were that of an enemy, they would not object to serving in their lodges rather than being all alone in the world.

Amana shouted, "I will not serve in anybody's lodge!"

"Don't be worried," Crow Woman said. "Perhaps they will be friends."

"And perhaps they are Assiniboins!" Amana snapped impatiently.

"*Aih!*" Grandmother Weasel Woman sighed. "That is possible. Those Assiniboins are the brothers of the Cold-Maker. Blizzards and cold nights do not bother them at all. They choose the coldest nights and the worst storms in which to prowl around and make trouble!"

"You worry unnecessarily!" Crow Woman exclaimed. "We are lucky tonight. Look! Even the moon has come out from behind the clouds to keep us safe."

The dark landscape suddenly gleamed as a glorious full moon appeared in the turbulent black sky.

The women were nearing a herd of animals, and they began to hear the bellowing of buffalo. The bulls uttered a long deep groan as they charged and fought among the bands of sprawling herds. Several times, as the three women hurried across the moonlit flatland, they approached a band of buffalo and startled them. The herd ran off—thundering over the hard ground, rattling their hoofs and snorting ferociously. Soon they vanished into the soft blue moonlight, but the women could still hear them running long after they disappeared.

Amana did not take her eyes from the remote campfire. As she and the grandmothers gradually drew closer to the distant blaze, she strained to hear just one word—anything that might identify the tribe of the strangers they were slowly approaching. But human voices could not penetrate the distant roar of buffalo or the howls of wolves that resounded mournfully in every direction.

They walked all night, and at daybreak they came in sight of a wide, dark gash in the great plain, which marked the course of the big river. Now they were moving along the broad trail worn in deep furrows by the travois and lodge poles of many camps of hunters traveling between the river and the mountains in the south. The sun was still new in the sky when at last they came upon the pine-clad rim of the flatlands and looked cautiously across the final knoll that separated them from the lodges and horses of the encampment they had seen from a distance. Although they were still far away, they could hear the noises of the morning camp, shouts, laughter, singing, and the beating of drums.

"*Aih*," Grandmother Crow Woman sighed, "that is good. I know these songs. It is the camp of our friends, the Gros Ventres."

As they trudged into the camp, they were stared at by everyone they passed. The chief's lodge was pointed out by an old man, and they approached it. Within there were several guests enjoying an early-morning feast and smoke. The chief, named Big Belly, motioned for the bedraggled women to be seated. He was a very grand, corpulent man, with a face full of kindness and concern for his exhausted guests.

After they had told their story of the terrible sickness, Big Belly gave them food, and he comforted them. He explained that many people of all the tribes of the region had died of the illness and that his camp was filled with the pathetically few survivors from whole bands that had been nearly destroyed by fever.

"You may stay with us," Big Belly offered. "But first you must rest, and then you may decide."

After eating and sleeping, Amana got up and left her grandmothers soundly sleeping in the safety of a widow's lodge and strolled through the camp. She sat by the stream that swept through the encampment and watched the girls and women fetching water and gossiping happily with one another. The boys splashed boisterously in the icy current. But Amana recognized none of her people among them.

When the sun was high, Amana returned to the widow's lodge, where an elder of the Gros Ventres was visiting Crow Woman and Weasel Woman. He was a big man with a great growth of hair, which he wore coiled on his head like a large knot. He was telling the old women that it was possible a few members of their band were among the people of the camp.

"How could this be?" Amana exclaimed.

"Many weak and pitiful people wandered alone for days until they collapsed and we found them lying in the flat-lands, with buzzards circling in the sky above them. Among these wretched survivors were a few of your people. Some of them died, but two of them are still living in the camp."

"I have spent the whole day looking for our people," Amana said, "but I found no one. There are none of our relatives here."

"You are mistaken," the man explained. "There is one lodge in which a man and woman live. The young woman was made into a monstrosity by the sickness, and the man is old enough to be her father though he says that he is her husband."

48

Amana was excited by this news. "Far Away Son was much older than SoodaWa! People often said he was old enough to be her father! Please tell me where we can find these people!"

No sooner had the man described the location of the lodge where the strangers lived than Amana ran headlong through the camp in search of it.

"Come out!" she shouted when she reached the dwelling. "I am one of your people! I have come to greet you!"

An urgent whisper came from the interior. "No . . . we cannot come out. Go away . . . we don't want to see anyone."

"You must let us see you!" Amana pleaded. "We are your own people. Crow Woman, Weasel Woman, and Amana."

There was a cry of surprise and remorse, and then the flap opened, and two strangers stood in the doorway of the lodge staring at Amana. The man was very old. His hair was white, and his face was lean and filled with sorrow. The woman also seemed old, though Amana could not be certain because she wore a robe over her head and hid her face behind her trembling hands. Neither of them spoke. They stood helplessly, peering at Amana as if they knew her.

"I am Amana," she said in the difficult silence.

The woman grasped her husband's hands and sank to her knees, sobbing. "Yes," she groaned, "you are Amana . . . and I am your sister, SoodaWa."

Two

It was in the winter that Amana was married.

A cold wind sprang up and swept among the lodges, bringing the smell of burning grass from the north. Amana had lived only twelve winters.

"I am old enough to be your sister's father," Far Away Son told her. "But it is the custom for a man to marry his wife's orphaned sisters. Do you understand?"

"Yes, I understand."

"SoodaWa is my sits-beside-me wife. And you will be my little child-wife. Do you understand what I am saying?"

Amana smiled.

The Cold-Maker had smothered the land with his deepest snow. While the men chopped holes in the frozen river and drew water for their horses, the boys ran through the camp in their buffalo-hide caps with big flaps to keep their ears warm, and shouted at the girls who huddled by their mothers in Hudson's Bay blankets and hair-lined mittens. When the blizzards had begun, Chief Big Belly had instructed his people to cut away the underbrush and some of the small trees so the lodges could be moved into the timber. The pines and firs made a good shelter against the great gusting wind and the drifting snow. There the people would remain for the winter, unless food became scarce, or there was not enough grass for the horses.

It was during this first storm that Far Away Son had told Amana she was to be married. He sat in front of her solemnly, his gray hair in long braids and a look of compassion on his ancient face. "Do you understand what I have told you, Amana?"

She gazed at his hands as he spoke and wondered if perhaps he might allow her to accompany him when he went hunting. He was such an old man. Surely he would need the help of someone young. SoodaWa was no longer young. The sickness had taken her life away. It had turned SoodaWa into a hag, stealing away her youth and her laughter. Now she walked slowly. Now she stayed indoors, crouching in the dimmest corner on the women's side of the lodge, and covering her face whenever anyone entered.

It was in that sad and long-ago winter that Amana was married.

Far Away Son sat quietly in the lodge, keeping track of

the days, making one notch on the counting stick for each moon. The old women, Crow Woman and Weasel Woman, kept Amana in their lodge before the marriage. They patiently explained to her the duties of a new wife, though Amana constantly interrupted their lessons.

"But will he let me go hunting?" she asked insistently. "Will he allow me to go on raids for horses? Will he let me fight?"

The grandmothers scolded Amana and begged her to accept Far Away Son's generous offer to make her his second wife.

"But will I have to cook and sew all the time?" Amana asked repeatedly. "And will I have to give up my dream of being a warrior?"

The grandmothers sighed. "Far Away Son is a man whose wife was crippled by the sickness. He is a man who needs a young woman to attend him. And you are the sister of his wife, and you must honor this good man who has offered to protect you and to care for you."

"I don't want to attend him!" Amana exclaimed, interrupting Crow Woman and waving her hands. "I don't want to be my sister's shadow!"

"But your sister dearly loves you," Weasel Woman said very quietly. "She had urged her own husband to marry you so you will have a good home. At this very moment she is making your marriage moccasins. How can you speak of SoodaWa with such anger?"

Tears suddenly came into Amana's eyes. "I had a dream," she whispered. "I had a dream of being someone special." Then she turned away and would not speak again.

When the blizzard turned out into the open plains and the camp was silent, the grandmothers tied a travois to the one horse they owned, a terrible old animal with a great sagging belly and swayback. Amana was given her bedding and two bundles, which were tied on the travois. One bundle contained dried meat, while the other was filled with the moccasins the old women had made for her. Then some blankets were loaded on top, and Amana was lifted onto the horse.

Amana cared nothing for the gifts or the travois. What fascinated and delighted her was being astride a horse. The man inside her wanted to ride away into the drifts of snow and never come back. But Amana would not let that strong man inside of her hold the reins. Today she had to be a woman.

She wore a buckskin dress, and her leggings were handsomely beaded. She was bundled up in a fine new blanket. And around her waist she wore a buckskin snake made for her by her grandmothers, to keep her childless. All these things the old women had given to her. And on her feet

Amana wore the beautiful moccasins that SoodaWa had made for her marriage.

Now Crow Woman and Weasel Woman reluctantly turned away. Amana awaited their return, but they did not come back. Night was coming, and the air was getting very cold. But still they did not return. Eventually a lone woman rode up on a chestnut horse and told Amana to follow her.

Amana desperately searched for her grandmothers, but they had disappeared. She cried out to them as the woman led her away. She begged them to come to her, but they did not respond. And soon the lodge of her grandmothers was lost in the darkness.

They crossed the entire camp until they came to the home of a man and his two young wives. When these people heard the arrival of guests, they came running outside and immediately took Amana down from her horse.

Amana turned away so they could not see her tears.

"What is the matter? You should be happy on the night of your marriage!" the younger wife said as she fed Amana.

"My necklaces—they are too tight," Amana lied, swallowing her sobs.

"You are a silly child!" the young wife snapped in a mocking voice. "I know what is the matter with you, little Amana. You would rather have some toys to play with than a new husband!"

Everyone in the lodge burst into boisterous laughter, and Amana felt she would either attack them or begin to weep uncontrollably.

But at that moment Far Away Son came into the lodge and suddenly everyone became respectfully silent, greeting the old man with great ceremony.

Far Away Son had come to fetch his young bride.

Amana gazed shyly at the old man as he approached. When their eyes met she sensed that he was as embarrassed as she, and at once they glanced away from one another.

He had brought heavy red cloth made in England and strings of many-colored beads, brass rings, silk handkerchiefs, Chinese vermillion, needles, thread, earrings, and an assortment of other exotic things that he had obtained from the trading post in the north.

Amana withdrew with a shudder of confusion and delight, wanting desperately to run away at the same time that she was overjoyed by the kindness of this old man who was her sister's husband. She wanted to embrace him and she wanted to hide from him. She wanted to leap so high into the night air that her breath would catch fire and she would become a star in the farthest heaven. She wanted to shout in rage and to cry for joy and to escape forever into the deep dark cave of her childhood. She wanted to be a woman of immense beauty and she wanted to be a man of great valor; a warrior of power and a holy woman of magnificent visions. But instead, she was living in the body of a child, standing helplessly in the center of a ring of complete strangers, while this gray, gray, wrinkled old man smiled self-consciously and stretched his gift-laden arms toward her beseechingly.

Amana could not move or speak. In her heart she could hear the voice of grandfather fox. But she could not understand his song. In her heart she could hear the dance of the foxes, but she could not move her feet to the beat of their drum. There was nothing but the crushing silence of the strangers all around her, nothing but a strange bitter happiness . . . until suddenly there was a sound.

Amana began to tremble as she peered around and saw the flap of the lodge slowly opening.

She groaned in fear. For in the doorway stood a huge owl. He blinked his yellow eyes. He placed his large hands upon his groin, and he smiled wickedly at Amana and said: "Come outside. I want you."

Amana screamed.

"My child, what is the matter?" came a voice.

Amana whirled around. There stood Far Away Son, his arms laden with gifts and a fragile smile upon his old lips.

Amana ran to him and hugged him around the neck, and he lifted her like a child and cradled her in his arms.

Then there was much joyful whooping in the wedding lodge as the old man, Far Away Son, carried off his child bride.

Before the river ice broke up, the Beaver Men held their ceremonies. After the long winter, they were anxious for spring. Their notched calendar sticks told them that the warm season was approaching. And when the geese were seen flying northward through the frosty morning sky, the people became restless. At last it was time to break their winter camp and roam the plains once again.

Soon the animals began to drift slowly away from the sheltered river valleys. Buffalo calves were born, just before the last great storm covered the trails.

Then, as suddenly, the snow melted and disappeared. These were the good days. The medicine-pipe ceremony was performed after the first thunder was heard in spring. The hunters killed the buffalo calves, and their skins were sewn by the women into children's robes and soft sacks. Spring was also the time for making willow backrests to refurnish the lodges. It was a good time.

Weakened by the long winter, the horses grew fat and strong on the sweet grass of spring; and the women dug bulbs, which they relished after the winter's diet of dried meat.

One evening a large herd of buffalo was discovered down beyond the bend in the river. The herd was so vast that the valley and the hills on each side of it looked like a great black sea. Even before camp was made, a group of young men prepared to go out and run the herd for meat. Amana gazed longingly at the buffalo and the hunters.

"We must set up the lodge," SoodaWa told her again and again. "Far Away Son is tired. He wants to lie down. Amana, are you listening to me? We must set up the lodge!"

Reluctantly Amana joined her sister, who hobbled painfully as she unloaded the travois and placed all the family's belongings in a neat pile on the ground. Then the two women laid out the tipi poles. SoodaWa already had the four main poles marked where they had to be tied. Amana unrolled the sinew and tugged at it as they knotted it around the poles. Far Away Son asked three young men to help the women lift the poles into the air and open them into a framework.

Then thirty poles were laboriously raised, one at a time. Finally, the last pole, the main one on which the tipi cover was fastened, was in place.

"*Aih!*" SoodaWa groaned. "It is not finished yet, Amana, so don't run away!"

When the cover was pulled around the structure, SoodaWa went inside and began spreading the poles apart so that the cover stretched tightly over the framework.

SoodaWa and Amana began circling the tipi, driving picket pins in at each place where there was a loop at the base of the covering. And at last they lifted the two final poles that were used to control the draft of the smoke hole on top of the tipi.

Amana lingered outside, peering with wonder toward the flatlands, where the sunset turned the hunters to bronze as they rode. How she wished to be astride a horse, flying through the air with those strong young men!

"Where are you now, Amana?" her sister called impatiently. "We are not finished yet. Must I do all the work by myself?"

"Ah!" hissed Amana under her breath. "Fish eater!" she cursed as she trudged back into the lodge, where SoodaWa was putting up the long curtain liner that was hung around the inside of the tipi to keep out the wind.

"Come along and help me with this," SoodaWa coaxed. "Don't be angry, Amana. I am no longer strong. I very much need your help, little one. And," she whispered self-consciously as she gazed at Amana, "I very much need your love."

Amana felt a rush of pity and shame. She hugged her sister. "I do not mean to hurt you, SoodaWa, but I have such a great storm within my heart," she said softly, "sometimes I cannot help the way I behave."

"I know . . . I truly understand. But we are alone now—just you and me and Far Away Son. You are all the family we have. And we must be gentle and help one another."

Amana nodded her agreement in a trace of confusion. SoodaWa was good and loving, but Amana felt trapped by her goodness and her love. And she felt ashamed that she could not become the person SoodaWa wanted her to be.

Amana could not describe the strong person inside of her. She could not speak of the great mystery that had come to her in the cave of the foxes. So she remained silent as she tied SoodaWa's best lining across the tipi where Far Away Son's bed would be placed.

"Look at these handsome backrests I have made," SoodaWa said as she set up the beds by laying down buffalo mattresses and then placing the willow backrests on their tripods at each end. "Aren't you pleased, Amana? Look at the lovely things I have made for our lodge."

It was true. SoodaWa's fingers were full of power. From them came marvelous colors and beautiful objects which she painted, sewed, and wove with a patience and concentration that was amazing to Amana. Amana could not make anything graceful with her hands. Everything came out wrong when she tried to follow her sister's careful instructions. There was no gift in Amana's fingers.

"Can you smell the fires burning, Amana?" SoodaWa asked. "Ah, what a good smell that is," she said happily. "And do you see how slow we are? We will be the last in the camp to light our fire . . . and the women will laugh at us."

"Their laughter doesn't bother me," Amana muttered as she stacked the rawhide containers full of dried meat and pemmican. "I'm not worried about what they think."

SoodaWa laughed. "Oh, but you are!" she said as she looked with a deep affection at her young sister. "You are like a little egg in a nest. The slightest tap, and you will break. Your problem, Amana, is that you care too much about everything." And once again she laughed as she hugged Amana.

When SoodaWa had set up her cooking tripod in the

center of the lodge, she said: "I think you have done enough work now. *Perhaps* you would like to go outside and watch the hunters."

Amana shouted and was gone even before SoodaWa had finished speaking.

Far Away Son was hobbling around the camp circle, announcing invitations to supper to various visitors who had news of survivors of the sickness.

"The Gros Ventres are nice enough people, and Chief Big Belly is a good man. But we need to rejoin our own tribe if we can find what has become of our people," he confided to Amana as she stood by the lodge, peering out toward the hunters, who were quickly approaching the herd of buffalo.

The men had already staked their saddle horses and let the ones that pulled the travois graze among the willows near the camp. All the elders were looking out toward the plains, where the young men were about to try their luck hunting the burly beasts that scattered as they approached them.

It was getting dark as the hunters charged in among the buffalo, splitting the herd. A thousand or so of the animals broke straight down the narrow valley toward the camp.

Down the valley the frightened buffalo lumbered, followed closely by the hunters. Amana was filled with such excitement that she let out a shout, and all the men around her followed her example. A resounding whoop went up as the great hairy beasts thundered toward them, sending up a whirlwind of dust that billowed and then spread out across the plains.

The lodges were pitched on the lower side of the bottom, between the river and a steep, rocky ridge. The roar of pounding hoofs burst against the bare rocks, bringing every man, woman, and child rushing outside to witness the chase. Amana clutched Far Away Son's wrinkled hand as the ground trembled. Then dust and grass flew into the air and there was a wind and a rattling of horns and a quaking of the earth as the beasts blindly charged past the camp.

The hunters' voices echoed in the rocks and across the river. Amana stared at the young men, their long glistening hair streaming in the wind as they carefully guided their horses among the sea of animals, singling out a fat cow or a choice young bull, firing their guns or leaning far away from their mounts and driving their arrows deep into the breasts of the great creatures.

Now the plain was filled with dust. Blood was on the tall grass. The buffalo stood trembling—heads down, swaying, staggering until they crashed to the ground in great panting heaps.

No one cheered the hunters. No one spoke.

This was a sacred moment. These great creatures were the food of all the tribes of the plains. It was they who provided every necessity of life. And their deaths were regarded with reverence and pity.

This silence was suddenly broken. The camp's saddle horses had been drinking quietly at the river, grazing among the willows, when all at once they galloped up the bank and raced out over the bottom in a panic, heads and tails held high. Blindly they ran toward the main herd of buffalo. The buffalo bolted and swerved eastward. For a moment they lurched, and then they came tearing down the valley. The rocky ridge hemming the camp in was too steep for them to climb, so the beasts just kept coming at full speed, directly toward the lodges.

People screamed, and children cried. The hunters shouted to one another, trying to head off the stampede.

Far Away Son seized Amana, but she pulled away from him and would not flee from the onrushing giants that suddenly came crashing through the camp. Far Away Son yelled to her as he and SoodaWa crouched behind their lodge. But she would not take her eyes from the beasts or the hunters. As they charged past her, she could smell their bodies, and she could see the fire of the stars in their little black eyes.

The people camped near the ridge clambered up along the jagged rocks. Those near the river leaped into the icy water. But many stood helplessly behind their lodges as the air filled with the bellow of galloping mad animals.

The buffalo made their way between the lodges, moving almost gracefully, nimbly jumping from side to side to avoid the obstacles in their paths, kicking and bucking as they

rushed past the anxious people. The people knew that anything might throw the herd into further confusion, making
them bunch up so they would overturn the lodges and
trample the people hiding behind them.

Finally the last of the buffalo passed beyond the outer
lodges, and the entire herd splashed into the river and crossed
to the opposite side, where a sudden and complete calm
overtook the animals.

No one had been hurt. Not a single lodge had been
overturned. But the long scaffolds of drying meat and many
hides and pelts pegged out on the ground to dry had been
thrashed into fragments.

Amana still stood silently in the spot where she had
remained during the stampede. And Far Away Son smiled
proudly when Big Belly murmured: "This child-wife of
yours is a very exceptional woman. Maybe she will bring
you luck."

The next morning the trees bordering the river were hung
with offerings made by the people to Sun in thanksgiving
for their survival. They gave their most cherished orna-
ments and their favorite household finery. No sacrifice was
too great for the sacred buffalo, who had swept through
the camp without harming a soul.

As the days passed, the nights became cooler. The sarvis
berries ripened. The long rays of the sun left the sky earlier
each evening. And the women, smelling the dry grass of

fall in the air, tried to put up as much meat, berries, and pemmican as possible. After they had finished making cold-weather clothing for their families, they continued to prepare buffalo robes for trading. These valued hides were taken by the leading men to the trading posts in the north, where they were exchanged for knives of metal, brass rings, tea, beads, rifles, ammunition, sugar, cloth, whiskey, mirrors, iron pots, and all the other new things the white men made.

"I'd like to see the new trading posts," Far Away Son mused while he sat smoking.

"Well," Amana whispered, "why don't we go!"

Far Away Son smiled and nodded.

SoodaWa hushed her sister. "Mind what you are doing and don't talk so much."

In the silence Far Away Son continued to stare off into space.

The women sat on the ground. SoodaWa had laid down a circle of stones. On this she made her open fire. On one side was a pile of firewood and on the other was dried meat, flour, baking powder, berries, potatoes, fat, sugar, salt, and tea. Without getting up she could keep the fire burning brightly, prepare the food, and cook it. She owned a piece of chain, which she fastened to the large wood tripod that stood over the fire. From the hook at the end of this chain she hung one of her cast-iron kettles that had come to her through many different hands across the prairie.

The lodge got very warm when SoodaWa was cooking.

"It is too hot," Far Away Son mumbled as he took up his tobacco board. "Why must it be so hot in here?"

"Why don't we go outside?" Amana exclaimed, without thinking that her sister needed her help. The old man liked the idea.

"Amana, be still!" SoodaWa said with a frown. "Sit down and give me the tea. How will you learn to cook if you are always running off with the men?"

Far Away Son grunted and resumed his position on the floor while Amana sighed in resignation.

"I don't know which of you is the bigger child," SoodaWa said with a faint smile.

While the water was beginning to boil, SoodaWa made tea. She always made the tea first. Then while the water boiled rapidly, she prepared the flour for making bannock bread. She kneaded a batch of dough, and then she greased her big frying pan with fat and spread the dough upon it very evenly. She placed the pan on a red-glowing bed of coals that she had scraped away from the fire, and she held it there until a wonderful aroma rose from the bread as it slowly browned.

"Don't let it burn," she whispered to Amana, giving her charge of the frying pan. "Watch what you're doing so I can be proud of you, little one. Show Far Away Son how good a cook you have become."

While Amana carefully watched over the bread, SoodaWa put potatoes and dried meat into the boiling water and hung it back over the fire.

"A band of Siksika told Big Belly that the Hudson Bay Company has a post over in the mountains where they trade gunpowder and white man's food for buffalo robes," said Far Away Son as he cut and mixed herbs on his tobacco board. "But Big Belly decided not to send anyone there, because it is too far."

Amana glanced anxiously at her sister. By Far Away Son's tone she knew that he wanted to visit the trading post.

"Perhaps . . ." Amana started to say.

"Mind the bread!" SoodaWa said, interrupting her with a look of exasperation.

"Yes, indeed," Far Away Son sighed without looking at either of his wives, "I would like to see one of those new trading posts of the French people."

"I am too weak to go such a distance," SoodaWa said. "And you are too old to travel by yourself."

"I could go!" Amana exclaimed suddenly. "I could go! I could cook for you, and I could watch over you, and I could help you!"

"Perhaps it is too long a journey . . ." Far Away Son murmured cautiously as he glanced at SoodaWa for approval. "And maybe you would need me to be here."

"*Aih!*" muttered SoodaWa. "Then go if that is what you have decided to do. Go and take the child, and let's be done with talking about it!"

Amana was jubilant. She hugged Far Away Son, and she kissed SoodaWa and pranced around in delight until even SoodaWa had to smile. "But you must dress warmly because it is cold in the mountains, and you must promise that you will return before it is time to break camp," SoodaWa said.

"Good," Far Away Son said happily. "Then it is decided. Amana and I will go."

"She is just a child," SoodaWa whispered as she served her husband his dinner. "She wants to be a grown-up, but she is still a little girl. Look at her! Everything is a game to her!"

"*So-kah-pi!* . . . Good!" Amana shouted, getting up and chanting at the top of her voice as she ecstatically danced out into the cold moonlight—her warrior's heart swelling with the secret song of the foxes.

"Come back!" SoodaWa called. "Come back, Amana, and sit down and eat and behave yourself, or I won't allow you to go!"

Amana came back into the lodge and politely took her place for dinner. She conducted herself with the restraint of a grown-up woman until her sister turned away to serve the bannock bread. At that moment she opened her mouth with a silent shout of joy. Far Away Son smiled happily at her.

During the days of preparation for the journey, Amana could think and talk of nothing but the wonders of the trading post. ". . . and I want to get a good look at those white people," she was saying as she packed pemmican in a rawhide box. She had seen only a few of the men at a great distance. But she had never been able to get close to one of them and really see what they were like. "And I'm especially anxious to see some of the white children and women," she continued in her breathless monologue, "and I want to see all the cloth and all the beads. I bet they have more kettles than I have seen in my whole life! . . . And more knives and more guns and more . . ."

"That's enough, little one," SoodaWa muttered as she loaded the travois. "None of us will have any peace until you are on your way!"

"Please," Amana pleaded with her sister, running to her and hugging her. "Don't be annoyed with me, SoodaWa. I beg you." And then she peered into SoodaWa's scarred and discolored face. "Please . . ." she whispered, "try to be happy for me. This is what I want more than anything else—just to have this one adventure."

SoodaWa turned away abruptly, sobbing as she hid her face behind her hands. "Don't look at me like that, little one," she murmured. "Don't look at me, Amana . . . because you will see how ugly I have become, and you will see why it is that our husband is like a father to both of us. You are too young and I am too ugly."

"But that isn't true," Amana wept as she buried her face in her sister's long hair. "You are such a good woman, SoodaWa. And your goodness is so beautiful! You are Far Away Son's sits-beside-him wife. He wants to give me toys and he wants to lift me upon his shoulders. But he looks at you sometimes as if you were more wonderful than anybody in the world!"

SoodaWa brushed away her tears and looked at Amana with a deep affection. "What is to become of you, little one?" she whispered, kissing her and smiling weakly. "And how is it possible that someone like me—someone as plain and simple as I am—and someone as strange as you . . . how is it possible that we could be sisters?"

"All I know and all I care about," Amana exclaimed, hugging SoodaWa, "is that I am going on a great journey to see the *apekwan* . . . the trading post! And if I should die after this trip I won't complain!"

"If you die?" SoodaWa laughed. "Yes, you will surely drop dead of old age at any moment—you are so decrepit! Yes, indeed, you will certainly die even before you get the packing finished if you keep talking so much!"

The sisters burst into laughter, gazing fondly at one another with glistening eyes. SoodaWa hugged Amana very tightly, as if the love she was feeling was so great it was painful. Then she whispered: "Do not hate your sister because she criticizes you. Try not to hate me, Amana. I want you to grow up to be beautiful. And I want you to be happy. Oh, how much I want you to be a good wife and mother. But even if you do not want to be a wife—and if you don't want to be a mother—then whatever it is you want to be, Amana, I say yes to it. Do you understand, little one? I say yes to you."

And they embraced one another again.

A few days later, as the sun came over the long shoulder of the rocky ridge behind the camp, the sisters bid each other a tearful good-bye. Amana lingered for a moment, looking at SoodaWa, trying to recall the handsome woman she had been before the sickness, trying to remember their father and mother before the terrible winter's night when the owl had brought them misfortune. But all the days before these bad times had vanished from her memory. The lost summers, the lost parents, and the vanished beauty of her sister made Amana deeply sad—a sadness that took hold of her heart and grew.

"Do this for me," SoodaWa mumured in her ear when she saw the sorrow flood into Amana's eyes. "Be beautiful and be strong! Do this for me, Amana. Do this for both of us!"

Amana leaped onto the handsome pinto that her sister had given her for the trip, and when Far Away Son had inspected the harnessing of the poles that bound the travois to his horse, he mounted and waved farewell to SoodaWa.

The morning sun rippled over the yellow grass of autumn that twisted in the steady breeze flying into their faces from the north. They rode along the ridge until they approached a sweep of country so wide and deep that it turned into sky in the distance.

As they rode along at a canter, Far Away Son shouted back to Amana: "I am going to show you the world of your ancestors!" And then he hooted happily as he stood up in his saddle and peered out over the luminous immensity that surrounded them. "And I am going to show you the white men. They are different from anything you have ever seen. They are not like the *Itey-skada*—the white foreheads who come to trade among us. The *Itey-skada* are half-breeds whose Indian mothers married the strangers. They have white foreheads because they always wear their hats in the sun. But the real white men are not like the white foreheads. They have made wonderful things that we do not have. But they have also made some bad things. You must beware of the food they eat. It will make all your teeth come out. *Wambadahka*—Look at this," Far Away Son shouted proudly. "My teeth are good—every one of them is perfect. But the teeth of our young people are no good. Too much white man's food. Our people, they never used to die until they were maybe a hundred summers old! Now, since we started trading skins for the white man's sugar and flour, we are sick all the time."

They rode quietly for a long time. Amana wanted to know more about white men, but Far Away Son was silent. Then, after they had stopped for water, he said, "So we trade our buffalo robes for blankets and gunpowder, but we do not take much of the food. They will try to get us to take more food than gunpowder, but we will be wise and gently refuse, so we do not make them angry. The traders are men with no respect for women, so you must be careful of them. They think nothing of taking advantage of an Indian woman; for they think of nothing but themselves and of the furs they want from us. Yet they truly have brought many remarkable things to our land. But for me, it is difficult to imagine that such men who have no regard for women or for the beauty of the land could make so many wonderful things. Sometimes I think they are very powerful people, and sometimes I think they are fools. They speak our language so badly, and they do not care about the proper ceremonies of meeting strangers or talking to the elders. They care nothing for our songs of destiny or the solemn power of the old ones. All they want from us is furs. They care for nothing else. And so we rob for them—stealing the coats of more animals than we can eat." And Far Away Son shook his head in dismay. "I am sad that we have become robbers, but I know that in the long winters we would starve without the things the strangers bring to us."

They continued to travel for six more days, always keeping close to the edge of the foothills. Then one morning, while they were breaking camp, one of the white foreheads came riding toward them, shouting salutations.

He asked Far Away Son who he was and where he was

going. Far Away Son explained with the language of his hands that they were the people of the Backbone of the World and that they had come to see the trading post.

The white forehead seemed disturbed by that announcement and asked Far Away Son to remain camped until he could ride into the trading post and assure the white men that they had come in peace.

"What does this crazy half-breed think?" Far Away Son muttered without taking his eyes off the brown fellow in white men's clothes. "Does he actually believe that a girl-child and a tired old man are going to make a raid on the trading post?"

Amana laughed, and her laughter made the white forehead nervous. He stared at the strangers apprehensively. Far Away Son saw the troubled look on the man's face, and using hand signs he quickly reassured him. They would stay camped where they were and patiently await an invitation from the white men to visit the trading post.

The white forehead did not waste any time turning back toward the trading post. Obviously he was frightened by the peculiar sight of a lone girl and man in the middle of the flatlands, and suspected that they might be some very clever decoy for a large band of raiders.

Far Away Son and Amana waited for two days. They knew that they were being watched. And they knew that the white men would not come near them until they were certain that they had come in peace. So they waited.

74

Finally the white forehead returned and told them that the white minister was coming out to visit them before they were allowed to enter the trading post.

When Far Away Son received this news he was delighted, for he had heard much talk of these black robes who were the holy men of the strangers. In order to welcome the minister properly, he told Amana to make tea while he painted his face and put on his best medicine clothes. In a short time the minister came hustling along in a narrow-wheeled little wagon, pulled by a handsome mare. He shook hands with Far Away Son, and then he began to talk in a strange language. He talked and he talked and all the while he continued to shake Far Away Son's hand.

Amana stared at the minister. He was the whitest creature she had ever seen. Even his hands were white. And all the hair was missing from his head.

He made gestures and he spoke very rapidly. Then he pretended that he was washing his face, and he pointed into the sky and put his hands on his breast and closed his eyes.

It was a most remarkable performance. The people of the plains rarely interrupt someone when he is talking, even if he should talk all day—which seemed likely in the case of this minister. So Far Away Son and Amana stood politely and listened and watched without understanding a word.

While the minister continued his sermon, the white forehead returned and said that the trading post was open. Far

Away Son realized that the preacher was not going to stop talking, so he began to back away very slowly, constantly nodding his head and trying to smile; until he and Amana had reached their horses, mounted them, and—still smiling and nodding—galloped away as fast as they could.

As they rode into the post they saw amazing things around them. There were stables full of hairless buffalo—curious beasts that smelled so terrible they had to cover their noses as they rode past. There were many wagons and very large dogs and a pole stuck in the ground with a decorated cloth flying from the top.

When they arrived at the house of logs, the traders came out to meet them. These white men spoke to Far Away Son through an interpreter whose skin was very black and whose hair was twisted into a mane as bristling and dark as the buffalo's. While they exchanged greetings Amana crept up behind one of them and tried to see what a white man smelled like. He had the same smell as milk, and it made her ill to be close to him.

The traders were surprised that Far Away Son had come without anything to barter, but they were polite to him and suggested that he tell all the people of the plains that they were welcome to bring their buffalo robes to the post, where they would receive more good things than from any other post of the region.

Then the visitors were invited to a feast, and much food was laid out. But Amana could not eat it. The tea had milk in it. On the bread was a grease that smelled like the hairless buffalo, and the meat was too sweet. She watched in astonishment as the pale men pushed this terrible food into their mouths. She watched as they chewed and swallowed.

After this the traders brought out many things and showed them to Far Away Son, keenly watching the expression on his face.

"Everything you could want is here at the post," they said through the interpreter. There was flour, molasses, bread, axes, cloth, necklaces, and curious things that Amana and Far Away Son had never seen before.

"And do you have balls and powder for our guns?" Far Away Son asked. The traders ignored his question and kept bringing out other things to show him. Far Away Son asked the interpreter where they kept their ammunition, and the black man pointed to a small wooden house. Without saying a word, Far Away Son turned from the traders and walked to the house and looked inside.

The interpreter rushed into the house and barred the way. "Nobody's allowed in here!" he barked.

Far Away Son smiled vaguely and looked past the traders at a large pile of black, shiny powder against the wall of the shed.

"Do you know what that is?" the trader asked through the interpreter. "That's gunpowder," he said with an angry look on his face. "And do you know that just a little bit of that powder will kill a deer?"

Far Away Son calmly nodded his head and kept peering at the big pile of black dust.

"Well, then," the trader muttered, "can you imagine what would happen if I should set off that whole pile? And that's exactly what I'm going to do if you start any trouble. I'll fire one shot into that stuff and kill the whole crowd!"

"*Ish-chim-ma-che*," said Far Away Son, glancing at the befuddled interpreter.

"What'd he say?" the trader demanded.

"He wants one of your wooden matches," said the interpreter.

"What for?" asked the trader.

"To light a match to the powder to see how good it is before he recommends it to his people."

The trader's face turned ashen. He tossed his box of matches to the interpreter, shouting: "Run, you damn fool! And don't stop till you get to the creek and have thrown those matches in the water!"

But before the interpreter could respond, Far Away Son laughed and said: "Stay. Tell the white man we people of the plains can make jokes too. Tell him that when we go to war we pull off our clothes and paint ourselves. We do not send our old men with little girls to make trouble. Now, let him tell us how much of this powder he would give our people for each buffalo robe—and then we will decide if we come back to your trading post."

The trader smiled when Far Away Son's words were

translated for him. "You tell your braves that we will give them a good bargain if they bring us good robes. You will leave our post with enough powder to kill all of your enemies on the prairies!"

Far Away Son grinned at Amana, who had been pressed to his side during the conversation. "These white men," he murmured, "are very concerned for our welfare. They always want to help us kill each other."

The leaves of the aspen flew in the wind, and the air was damp and full of moths as they returned to the camp between the river and the ridge. The summer hunt was over, and the women were preparing for the journey to the winter settlement. It was a time of gray skies and sad farewells as the tribe split into small bands that ventured alone into the winter's landscape, where food was no longer sufficient to support a large population. So each band had to fare for itself and work hard to survive the hardships of the cold season, until at last it was summer once again and the bands reassembled on the open plains for the great tribal buffalo hunt.

The women had been awake and working hard since dawn. They had prepared the breakfast and finished packing, and were taking down the lodges. The scouts had moved out ahead of the caravan assembling behind the medicine-pipe owner and Big Belly and the other chiefs.

There were many shouts and greetings for Far Away Son and Amana as they rode into camp. The people were falling in line behind the chiefs in family groups with their travois, pack animals, saddle horses, and the herds of horses of each owner. These beasts were driven by the older boys. The babies rode on their mothers' backs in the folds of buffalo robes. And the bigger children rode on the travois, contentedly clapping their hands and giggling as they bounced along. The older girls were bunched up two and three on a horse, clinging to each other and talking, while their mothers rode beside the men on the horses pulling the travois.

Far Away Son and Amana were happy to see the people of the camp, but when they came upon their lodge they discovered that nothing had been done to prepare it for the departure of the band.

Crow Woman hobbled out to them before they could dismount. She was crying. SoodaWa was very ill.

"She has fallen down," Crow Woman said. "Soon after you left she fell to the ground and she seemed dead for three days. Then she opened her eyes. But she could not talk and she could not stand." The old woman wept as she embraced Amana and led her into the lodge. They found Weasel Woman sitting on the ground and praying beside the stricken SoodaWa.

When SoodaWa saw Far Away Son, her eyes brightened slightly and she seemed to sigh. But she could not lift her head nor clasp his hand when he knelt over her and whispered: "*O-ke nik-so-koo-wa* . . . Hello, my friend. I am here with you now."

Amana covered her face and turned away. For a moment she trembled helplessly, but then she took a deep breath and said in a flat, determined voice: "Why are you weeping instead of preparing for the winter's journey? What is the matter with both of you? We cannot stay here by ourselves. We must hurry and get ready before the caravan leaves us behind!"

The grandmothers nodded in confusion and glanced anxiously toward Far Away Son for his instructions. But he was silent, bowed over his wife, whispering to her.

"Did you hear what I said?" Amana exclaimed impatiently. "Come along," she shouted as she helped Weasel Woman to her feet. "I will help you. It is not such a great task to take down a lodge. Two of us can do it quickly. But hurry and stop crying. SoodaWa will die if we get left behind!"

While Amana shouted orders, the lodge and all its contents were hurriedly packed and readied for the departure. And when Big Belly finally raised his arms to the sky and asked the blessings of Sun, Amana gently touched Far Away Son and gestured for him to help carry SoodaWa to the travois they had prepared for her. The old man had tears in his eyes as they secured the feverish body among the furs. Then, while SoodaWa's eyes gazed fixedly into the sky, the caravan began to move.

The day's march ended in the late afternoon, giving the women time to set up the lodges, unpack the horses, and prepare the evening meal before dark. Big Belly had chosen a good campsite, and he had already selected the place for his own lodge. Now all the families were pitching their tipis around that of Big Belly in an uneven cluster. Horses whinnied as the boys took them to graze; dogs whined at the smell of the evening meal cooking, and people shouted to one another in the cold evening that was filling the overcast, turbulent sky.

Amana peered down at SoodaWa and gently wiped the perspiration from her scarred face. "Can you understand me?" she whispered.

The eyes came momentarily to life and seemed to acknowledge her question.

"Rest," Amana murmured. "I promise you I will take care of everything. This is what I promise you, SoodaWa."

In the morning it was raining. The drops pelted the lodge covering, turning it into a drum upon which the wind and rain played a sad melody. It was too stormy for the band to travel, and so Big Belly sent the camp crier to announce that they would not break camp that day. Amana lay awake on her couch, listening to the chanting of Far Away Son, whose prayers mixed with the song of the rain and came to her from across the lodge.

SoodaWa had shuddered and groaned all night. Amana was not able to sleep and had sat up with her sister, dripping water over her lips and wiping the deluge of sweat that poured from her body. By morning SoodaWa was quiet and her fever was gone.

"You must sleep now, Amana," Far Away Son told her when he awakened. Then he sat down by his wife with terrible grief on his face.

Amana nodded aimlessly and did what she was told, creeping wearily to the other side of the lodge and curling up on her damp couch. But she could not sleep. The chanting of Far Away Son and the music of the rain filled her with dread. Everything had changed. Everything seemed different to her. She ran her hands over her body and could not recognize it. It was someone new. Someone with breasts and supple hips. It was the body of a stranger in which she lived. And she began to weep. Perhaps she was crying for SoodaWa, perhaps for her old husband, Far Away Son. Or for herself. She did not know. She knew only that this winter would pass and another summer would come, and then another and another. She knew only that the sorrow in her heart had become so immense with her sister's illness that it had awakened a new person inside of her, a strong person like the warrior but a person full of gentleness and compassion. It was someone entirely new. Someone strange and soft, the kind of person SoodaWa had been.

Amana wept. She wept, and she vowed that she would be a good wife and she would look after her sister.

Amana reached into one of the boxes beside her bed and gently laid her fingertips upon the medicine bundle containing the regalia of a warrior and the bow—and the little drum that knew the songs of the foxes. And then she closed her eyes and she wept for them too.

Three

Moisture hung in the air. It was the warmest time of the summer. The moon was hidden by the great clouds of smoke that for days had tumbled over the mountains, caused by vast forest fires on the other side of the Backbone of the World. The stench and fumes were so thick they burned the nostrils. Ash lingered in the windless sky. And SoodaWa sat on her couch while the grandmothers fed her like a child, wiping her chin and patting her on the head when she made a little groan of complaint or an equally small expression of contentment.

She had lain upon her couch for many seasons, and she had gradually recovered enough strength to sit up and feebly nod her head when she wanted something. But she would never be able to care for herself again. She had died in the middle of her life, and what remained was an old woman, more helpless than Weasel Woman or Crow Woman.

The only timber in the little valley was three huge cottonwood trees. One of them, a sprawling giant, had been blown down long ago, and from its brittle bare limbs Amana replenished the fire. Then she sat down with a great sigh and stared into the flames.

Far Away Son did not often remain in his lodge. The sorrow there was too great a burden for an old man, and so he feasted and smoked with Chief Big Belly and the other elders. They talked about the time of the Sun Dance, which was quickly approaching—the climax of the summer days. All the young men had left the camp for the tribal hunt that had been organized by the men's societies. Soon they would return with the sacrificial food essential for the Sun Dance. As many as three hundred bull tongues were needed; so the hunters had been away from the camp for many days.

Far Away Son was not a religious person. He was a follower of the religion of his people, but he had never joined any of the secret societies. He always attended rituals, and he recounted his coups in the main medicine lodge, but he had little interest in spiritual matters. He was a very practical man. The other elders frowned upon this neglect, but Far Away Son's proven abilities as a hunter and warrior outweighed any prestige lost because of his indifference to religious life.

"You are a scoundrel," Big Belly laughed, "but no one is better at raiding for horses and nobody tells better stories about the old days!"

"And besides," one of the elders of the Horns Society said, "you have many troubles, my friend. A wife who is too ill to be a wife and a wife who is too young to be a wife."

The men snickered quietly. Far Away Son was being mocked. But he did not care. He loved SoodaWa. And he had come to admire Amana for her strength and good sense. "An old man," he told his young wife, "does not need a woman as much as he needs a sister and a companion."

This touched Amana. She kissed Far Away Son on the head. "I also do not need or want a lover," she whispered. "I cannot understand why I am different from other women, but you have made me feel good. And you have made me feel strong." She kissed the old man again, and she hung the kettle over the fire to make tea while Far Away Son knelt by SoodaWa and smiled at her and stroked her hands again and again.

"Those old men know only what their fathers did. I know what I have done," Far Away Son exclaimed with a triumphant gesture as he sat down on his couch and sipped tea. "I am too old to worry about what people think of me. I do not need the men's societies to tell me who I am. I know who I am! And that is the way I have been all my life," he declared. "And that is why it is good that you are my wife, Amana . . . because we are both independent." He laughed in a croaking voice.

"Get your sister," Far Away Son went on happily, "and

bring her here to me, and then we will all go outside and sit by the creek before we suffocate in this terrible summer's heat!"

"SoodaWa is not well enough to go out," Amana cautioned. "Let her sleep where she is on her couch by the fire. The heat is good for her."

The old man grunted in agreement and stumbled into the evening. Soon the grandmothers and Far Away Son were hobbling toward the water's edge, where they sprawled under the wide limbs of the cottonwood tree and comforted each other with memories.

"And what will you do?" Far Away Son called to Amana when she came to the creek to fetch more wood for the cooking fire.

"Yellow Bird Woman is coming here to talk with me," she replied. "She has many problems, and I am the only one she trusts."

"She has good sense!" Far Away Son exclaimed. "She is a good woman and her husband, old Looking Back, is far too ugly to have such a pretty young wife! Just as I am!"

Far Away Son and the grandmothers laughed in the hot summer night.

Looking Back was indeed fortunate, for Yellow Bird Woman was exceptionally handsome, and she was concerned and interested in her lodge and her duties. She was devoted to her works as a wife. But she was a dreamer. She longed for romance as intensely as Amana longed for adventure. The two young women understood each other's dreams, though the life each wanted was very different. Yellow Bird Woman and Amana often sat close together and stroked and kissed each other sorrowfully as they talked about the disappointments and desires they could share with no one else.

Yellow Bird Woman had not wanted to marry an old man. And she knew a young hunter who gave her much attention despite the danger of flirting with another man's wife.

"*Ma-che-ye-num!*" she whispered to Amana with the sparks of the cooking fire gleaming in her eyes. "Good-looking! And tall and possessing many fine horses! When he looks at me I cannot turn away. I try—but I cannot turn away from him, Amana!"

Yellow Bird Woman had been meeting Two Stars secretly, and she stayed with him when her old husband was away from his lodge with the members of his society.

Amana loved Yellow Bird. She loved to be with someone else who was young and in whom she could confide the adventures she dreamed about. Tonight she waited for her eagerly as always.

"*Aih!*" Amana murmured happily as she saw her friend hurrying across the encampment toward her lodge.

"*Shhhh!* . . . Be still, my friend," Yellow Bird Woman whispered when she came inside the tipi. She glanced over to be certain that SoodaWa was asleep. Then she sat next to Amana and whispered, "This is the last time we will see one another, my friend! Two Stars and I are running away as soon as the men return from the hunt!"

"No . . . no! You must not do it, Yellow Bird Woman! If you are caught they will punish you!"

"If I can be with him I don't care about punishment!" she exclaimed, a look of excitement flashing across her handsome face. "But they will never catch us. Two Stars is clever. He has arranged for us to join the Blood band in the north. We will be together and we will be safe!"

"I tell you, my friend, you risk everything doing this!"

"Please, Amana," the girl pleaded. "Kiss me and tell me that you will miss me and that you will never again have as good a friend as Yellow Bird Woman!"

Amana shook her head hopelessly. Now she understood how difficult it had been for SoodaWa. "You are a little fool," she murmured. "You are the same kind of fool that I used to be—full of impossible dreams and stubbornness!" She hugged Yellow Bird Woman and said, "If SoodaWa and Far Away Son didn't need me, I would run away and become the person who still lives quietly inside of me . . . so quietly that sometimes I am afraid he has died."

"*Aih!*" the girl exlaimed with relief. "You understand! *Aih*, I am so happy, Amana, because you have not told me to be sensible and to stay here and be content to live with old Looking Back!" Yellow Bird Woman threw back her head and smiled with great happiness. And then all at once

Amana felt old and useless and plain. "Ah," said Yellow Bird Woman when she saw the expression of sorrow fill her friend's face, "do not be sad because I am leaving, Amana. It is different for you. You don't want a lover. You are happy here with Far Away Son. You want to be a warrior and a hunter, and Far Away Son lets you do whatever you please. You don't care about love. You ignore Red Tail and the other good-looking young hunters who follow you to the river. I have seen you drive Red Tail away with a glance. He was so mortified that his love for you has turned to hatred now. But I am not like you, Amana. I can't help myself! I don't know what I would do if I had to spend all the rest of my life like you—taking care of your sister and sitting every night with an old husband who grunts and snores and smells bad! I can't do it, Amana! You must forgive me for being selfish. Two Stars promises to take good care of me and never to abandon me. He has promised me, Amana. He's so talented and fine! Have you seen how he dances with such spirit! There is no one his age who is as brave and no one as eager during the hunt. Tell me, please tell me that you like him and that you think I am not being a fool!"

Amana was depressed. She silently kissed Yellow Bird Woman, and then she sat back staring at SoodaWa, who slept fitfully on her couch on the other side of the lodge. Soon she too would be old and feeble like SoodaWa. Soon her dreams would drift away, leaving nothing but the kettle and the groans of uneasy sleep. Soon her only friend would be gone, and then one day her husband and her poor sister would die. And then she would be alone. Amana shuddered with the thought, for a woman without a family was a shadow, a beggar, and a stranger in every lodge. She shuddered again and tears came into her eyes.

"My friend," Yellow Bird Woman whispered, "I have made you sad!"

"No . . . no, it isn't you," Amana explained with difficulty, wiping away her tears and kissing Yellow Bird Woman urgently. "It is not you . . . it is everything here. . . ." Then Amana shook her head and took a deep breath as she tried to raise her spirits. "In the old days it was different, Yellow Bird Woman. We had the love of our people and the wealth of all the land as far as we could see. There was no sickness and starvation and sorrow. We lived in the dreamtime and each thing rested upon the other. But now we must struggle so hard to survive. Each of us must fight so hard to be happy. And sometimes I am afraid that I will not be able to fight. Sometimes I fear that I will give up and nothing will be left of me."

For a moment Amana did not speak. She gazed at her friend, and then she nodded her head and said, "I do not know—I really don't know what is right and what is wrong. I love you and I shall miss you. And I admit that it saddens me to lose my only friend. I wish that I still had your daring. I envy your daring, Yellow Bird Woman. But I also fear for you . . . for what will happen if the men catch you! All these things . . . this sadness and this envy and the fear confuse me." Amana wept. "But," she said solemnly as she looked into her friend's eyes, "all I can tell you is something SoodaWa said to me long ago when she was still strong and young. I don't know if what you are doing is right, but whatever you do and whatever you are, Yellow Bird Woman, I say yes to it. I say *yes!*"

The young women embraced, and Amana whispered, "We must not wake my sister. Let's go out by the trees with Far Away Son and the grandmothers. It's too hot to stay indoors."

Yellow Bird Woman went out into the brilliant moonlight. But Amana lingered behind for a moment, trying to recall the song of the foxes.

The melody had vanished from her memory.

She watched her young friend whose happiness filled her body with a bright dancing energy. Amana could not help being jealous of Yellow Bird Woman's beauty and gaiety. Her beauty was intensified by her great love, giving her power and grandeur. Amana felt powerless and empty. *"If only I were daring again!"* Amana murmured to herself as she pressed her hands to her breasts. If only she could open herself to another person as Yellow Bird Woman opened herself to her lover. How good it must feel to be loved. "How I wish I did not have to spend my life taking care of people . . . and feeling guilty whenever my thoughts

wander and whenever I long for something I cannot seem
to find. . . ."

But she could not recall the song of the foxes.

Amana stood silently by the lodge and watched Yellow
Bird Woman as she entertained the old people with a song.
"Oh, I am thinking . . ." Yellow Bird Woman was singing,
caring nothing that her song was scandalous.

> *Oh*
> *I am thinking*
> *Oh*
> *I am thinking*
> *I have found my lover*
> *Oh, yes*
> *I think that it is so!*

At last the hunters returned to the camp. The people
gathered happily, and there was a big feast of the favored
parts of the buffalo, the brains and kidneys. And everyone
also dined on the wild turnips the boys had gathered. Then
the women began to cure the meat the hunters had brought,
making many boxes of pemmican for the winter.

One evening the elders compared their calendar sticks
with one another, to determine the time of the Sun Dance.
At council it was decided to begin the journey northward
to the place of the holiest ceremony of the people. Camp

was broken, and early in the morning the caravan began its long trek across the river valleys. Within a few days Amana could see the vast Sun Dance camp spread out high above them on the broad, sunny flanks of the Tallow Flats, where for many ages the people had sent their young men through the rituals of thanksgiving and sacrifice.

It was a marvelous sight. And Amana called to SoodaWa: "Can you see it? Can you see how many lodges there are this year?"

The massive camp was filled with countless brightly painted tipis arranged in a huge circle. In the middle was the Sun Dance lodge, set up and awaiting the days of the dancing, when it would be enclosed in evergreens.

Now Amana and her family were passing among great numbers of sleek, wild-eyed ponies that had been turned loose to graze on the immense bald prairies. These handsome animals pranced stiff legged in circles, their tails raised and their heads high.

When the people of the camp saw the caravan coming in the distance, some of the boys jumped on their horses and galloped out to meet the newcomers, yelling as they rode, "*Hie, hie, hie, hie!* . . ." They led Big Belly and his people to the ground that had been set aside for their camp.

By the time Amana and the grandmothers had set up the lodge and arranged the couches, it was already dark. SoodaWa and Far Away Son were exhausted from the journey, and Amana promised to make tea for them. While she was boiling the water, there was suddenly a piercing shriek. Everyone sprang up and ran ouside. The men grabbed their weapons, thinking that some enemy was attacking the Sun Dance encampment. But it was Yellow Bird Woman who was screaming. Her husband had caught her as she was eloping with Two Stars.

At once news of the scandal swept through the camp. Everyone whispered as Looking Back seized his young wife and dragged her to the lodge of Big Belly. From the entrance of his lodge Far Away Son exclaimed, "What has she done? What is all the screaming?"

"Hush!" Amana whispered with dread. "Something terrible is going to happen to her!"

The camp crier announced a council in Big Belly's lodge. And he recited the names of those requested to be present.

Amana stood silently in the doorway, staring out into the deserted campground. One by one the old men walked solemnly to the chief's lodge. Then a fearsome silence settled over the village.

"Come . . . sit down with us, Amana, and have tea," Far Away Son urged.

But she would not leave the doorway.

"These Gros Ventres are good to their women," he assured her. "They will probably give her a good thrashing . . . just to disgrace her. And then everybody will go home glad that it was not they who got caught!" Far Away Son said.

"Hush!" Amana begged as she clung to the door pole and strained to hear the distant voices of the elders that hummed through the silent camp.

Then suddenly the crier's voice shouted: "Women! All women! Come to the lodge of Chief Big Belly!"

Amana still did not move. Her old husband watched her intently for a long while, and then he whispered, "You must go, Amana, or there will be much gossip. You will be ridiculed if you don't do what they tell you to do."

But still she would not move.

"Amana!" Far Away Son shouted angrily. "Do what you are told!"

"*Aih!*" she exclaimed, turning on the old man fiercely and shouting, "I will not do it! Do you hear me? I will not watch someone I love being beaten and humiliated!"

SoodaWa urgently thrashed her arms, reaching toward her sister, but Amana would not be silent.

"No! I will not! I will not obey simply because I am a woman! No! I will not do it! It is savage. It is wrong!"

"They will come for you," Far Away Son muttered. "I will not be able to protect you, Amana. They will come for you and drag you to the council."

Amana covered her face and nodded sadly, "*Aih* . . . you are right, they will come for me. And you will not protect me. And so what good is it to be a woman?" And then she glanced at her husband defiantly. She sat down near SoodaWa and gently took her hand. She smiled into her frightened sister's face. And then she looked at her husband and said, "So tell them I am not really a woman. That's what they think anyway. Tell them that I have never slept with my husband, and that I am only pretending to be a woman. But also tell them that I will not watch Yellow Bird Woman being punished!"

Few of the women wanted to go to the council, but the members of the men's societies went from lodge to lodge and ordered the women out. As the flap of Far Away Son's tipi was raised, Amana closed her eyes and squeezed her sister's hands.

"Come," the man demanded, peering inside. "Come now and hurry! The sick one may stay on her couch, but the other one must come. Hurry up! Didn't you hear the call?"

Amana shuddered as the man reached for her. But Far Away Son calmly stayed the fellow's hand. "She is not a Gros Ventre," he said quietly, though anger flashed in his old eyes. "She is my wife. And I am a stranger that your Chief Big Belly calls friend. My wife will not go."

The man paused with uncertainty. He was about to object, but then he turned away and dropped the door flap without saying a word. Amana gasped and began to weep.

"What a fool these women make of me . . ." Far Away Son groaned. "We will not be welcome among the Gros Ventres for very long."

His comment made Amana cry all the more, for she realized how much she loved the old man. He sat down by her with a sigh and stroked her hair, looking at her with a little smile. Then he said, "Well, we have been away from our own people too long anyway. If these Gros Ventres could survive the sickness, then there must be many more of our own tribe still living! Isn't that right?" He laughed so fondly that Amana kissed him and brushed back his gray hair. "Perhaps in this very Sun Dance camp—among all these many lodges—there are now some of our people!" he continued. "Yes! That's possible . . . right here in this camp! And tomorrow I am going to find out if some of our old friends are here and if they will take us with them when the Sun Dance is over!" Everyone was filled with renewed hope and happiness. And Far Away Son looked pleased. "What do you think of that?"

"I think," murmured Amana, ". . . that you are a good husband for a very crazy wife."

Suddenly the camp was filled with screams. Amana cried out and shuddered as she ran to the doorway. Once again there was a deep silence in the night that surrounded the luminous lodges. Nothing happened for a long time. Then the women mournfully dispersed from the meeting. The men followed silently, returning to their homes. And finally, when the campground was deserted, a lone figure staggered into the doorway of the council lodge. It swayed there for a moment, wailing. "*Aih* . . ."

Amana whimpered and cringed in agony when she heard the broken voice of her friend gasping in the distance, groan-

Jamake Highwater

ing as she blindly stumbled to the river, where, alone on the bank, she washed the blood from her battered face.

Amana started to run from the lodge without thinking, but Far Away Son caught her by the arm and, using all his strength against the urgent efforts of his wife, would not allow her to go to Yellow Bird Woman.

"Listen to me," he begged Amana. "I have defended you. I have done everything possible to spare you the pain of watching your friend humiliated. But now you must spare me the anger of Chief Big Belly, for if you go out there now in defiance of custom, and if you console your friend, then surely there will be terrible trouble for all of us."

Amana shook her head as she continued to tug against her husband's grip. "No, no," she sobbed. "I cannot just desert her."

"Listen to me, Amana," Far Away Son repeated.

She turned to him with agony in her eyes. She looked at him with such beseeching eyes that he too began to weep, but he would not let her go. Eventually, little by little, she became silent, and she ceased to pull against his grip. She sank slowly to the ground and covered her ears so she would not hear the long, low wail of the dark figure crouched on the riverbank.

All night pairs of warriors wrapped in a single blanket, with arms around one another's shoulders, strolled out into

100

the dark prairies, chanting the dolorous song of the Sun Dance. All night these brothers of the blood prayed for one another. *"Heh-h-h . . . heh-h-h . . ."* All through the starry night came the humming of the sacred song of male comrades. But there were no women's songs.

Amana lay awake and wept. She could not sleep. Every time she closed her eyes, she recalled the screams of her friend, and she would begin to weep again. No matter how hard she tried to put the sound out of her mind, it lingered there while the moon moved into the sultry sky and she could hear the constant padded step of moccasined feet outside her lodge as pairs of young men made their way through the darkness to mysterious destinations.

"Aih . . . aih . . ." SoodaWa whispered again and again to comfort Amana. But nothing could comfort her.

"I know what they have done to her," Amana groaned.

"Aih . . . aih . . . it is not true, little one. They gave her a beating . . . they only gave her a beating," SoodaWa intoned softly.

"I know what they have done . . . in the moonlight I could see what they did to her beautiful face." And she closed her eyes to try to force away the terrible image in her mind. But the blood and the battered face would not go away.

"Aih . . . aih . . ."

Far Away Son snored peacefully as he lay next to SoodaWa. A soft wind brushed past the door of the lodge, and Amana lay on her back, wide awake, looking up at the deluge of stars that shone through the smoke hole.

"How free men are!" she whispered. "How marvelous all the secrets they share!"

She raised the side of the tipi and cautiously peered outside. She could see several tall, blanketed figures creeping through the dark camp, bearing some secret ceremonial object between them. Moving silently with grace and power until they were gone. And now all that remained was the soft, distant sobbing of Yellow Bird Woman.

It was called the year of the mild winter, *itsa-estoyi*. That was how the people named the days that followed the Sun Dance. It was an easy time. The ground was bare of snow and the weather was unusually gentle except for an occasional storm which passed abruptly, leaving its fragile covering of ice to melt quickly and trickle away into the sunny brooks. The women of the camp did not have to break holes in the ice in order to draw water from the river, and the grass was already deep and green. So the women were happy and had much time to gather among the grazing horses and dream or gossip or pray for blessings for their children. But the men were worried.

There were no buffalo.

The band had drifted peacefully into their winter camp and waited patiently for the snow to drive the buffalo herds toward the foothills. But instead of blizzards and snow, the prairie was swept by great fires that roared across the dry land, leaving behind a black, barren waste where nothing could live. And so the buffalo did not come to them.

By the time Chief Big Belly realized the predicament of his people, many of them were already starving.

The chief came to the lodge of Far Away Son. "*O-ke* . . ." he said. "You people of the north know about the winter. So I have come to you to talk about a problem that makes us grieve. I can see you are better prepared than we are for this dry winter of fires, because your women do not groan with hunger and you have not complained that your belly is empty." With this, the chief laughed drearily and took the place of honor that was offered to him.

But Amana and the grandmothers did not smile, and SoodaWa lay upon her couch breathing slowly with open eyes and mouth.

Far Away Son greeted the chief cordially, and then he muttered, "Hurry, Amana. You must cook a meal for our guest." He smiled pleasantly and rubbed his hands together as he talked with the chief.

Amana sighed as she found three small potatoes and put them in the boiling water. The grandmothers fetched with trembling hands the morsel of dried meat that remained of their winter stores. And with squinting eyes they handed the meat to Amana and watched expectantly as she dropped it into the kettle.

"It is all we have," Crow Woman mumbled with down-cast eyes.

At this Far Away Son broke down. He covered his face and was ashamed. "It is the truth," he said haltingly. "We have nothing. There is no meat in our lodge. We have survived because we have eaten *fish*. I am ashamed because fish is forbidden to us, but we are hungry and SoodaWa is starving. And so we have tried to eat the filthy food. But it is like eating our own waste. It sickens us and gives us no strength."

"*Aih*," Big Belly groaned, raising his hand in refusal when Amana placed the food in front of him, "I do not mean to do you an offense by refusing your hospitality, Far Away Son; but it is the same with you as it is with all of us, and so I cannot take your food while so many of my people are starving."

The chief left the lodge, and at once he ordered that the camp be prepared to move. And in the morning the hungry people started out over the blackened plains in search of the shaggy creatures that alone could give them back their lives. They did not find them until they had reached the eastern limits of their hunting grounds. There, dangerously close to the Cree, Assiniboin, and Sioux, they camped for their winter hunt.

For those who endured this long journey there was food. But en route to the buffalo, many of the people had died.

Grandmother Weasel Woman, groveling blindly for grubs

and roots, perished soon after they started across the windless cinders of the flatlands. Amana had cut up rawhide boxes and saddles and boiled the leather, but the old women refused to take nourishment away from SoodaWa, who lay dead except for her steady panting. They searched the ground for something to eat. Crow Woman pressed her digging stick into the barren earth, but even the grass roots had shriveled and died in the fire. And so one morning Grandmother Weasel Woman did not wake up.

The next to die was old Looking Back, husband of Yellow Bird Woman, who wept for the old man she had never loved, the old man who had killed her lover. She came to Amana, who embraced her friend and would not let her go.

"No, do not look at me, Amana," Yellow Bird Woman sobbed. "I have lost everything . . . my beauty is gone, my lover is dead, and now this old man who was my husband has left me to starve. I have no family, and men will not take pity on a woman whose face is marked like mine!"

Yellow Bird tried to run away, but Amana would not let her go. She looked imploringly at Far Away Son.

The old man sighed and nodded with a look of grief and pity in his face. "We have nothing," he said as he crouched numbly over the prostrate body of SoodaWa, "but you may come here to us, Yellow Bird Woman, and be the friend of Amana." And then tears came into the old man's eyes as he looked at his young wife. "Look at Amana," he intoned in a wail, "already she is getting old from this hardship. She is surrounded by nothing but old people who can do nothing to help her. Perhaps you can make these bad days better for your friend, Yellow Bird Woman. So you are welcome here."

Amana was delighted, and she embraced her husband and then she ran back to Yellow Bird Woman, and she laughed with tears in her eyes.

"You see," Amana exclaimed, "we shall still be friends, you and I; and no one will be unkind to you again!"

But the young widow was mad. She wept from hunger. She crouched in a corner and covered the gaping scar on her face, and she begged for food from anyone who passed the lodge. Her beauty was gone, and with it her sanity vanished. The hunters ridiculed her, and the women scolded her when she took morsels of food from the children. What remained of Yellow Bird Woman was a weeping, helpless creature.

As the days passed, Amana slowly pulled away from her friend and gazed at her with enormous regret. The marvelous young girl whose exuberance and daring had delighted Amana was gone. The humiliation and disfiguration had taken away her mind. Now she only whimpered from behind her hands.

Hunger brought out the most feeble character of the entire family. The lodge was constantly filled with complaints and the sound of weeping. Far Away Son was helpless from fatigue, and the women argued bitterly over the smallest problem. It was a bad time. Death circled the camp tirelessly, and one by one, the people wandered off into the darkness and never returned.

Then one morning Amana took her husband's rifle and walked out of the lodge in silence—the song of the fox came suddenly into her heart. She knew that she would have to find something for her family to eat if any of them were to survive. But the land where they camped on their eastward journey to the buffalo was lifeless and filled with nothing but other pathetic members of her band, who scratched among the clods of dirt or ran recklessly into the clouds of cinders in pursuit of some tiny animal that had wandered out into the black desolation.

She walked and she walked until her moccasins and legs were covered with soot. The air was cold, but the sky was empty. No rain. No snow. Just an infinite succession of black dust devils rising out of the bleak land.

Then when she was about to turn back, she saw something move. Instantly she whirled around and took aim. The creature loomed clearly in her sights for just a moment.

It was a fox.

Amana could not pull the trigger. She opened her mouth and let out one long wail as her rifle followed the fleeing creature. But she could not shoot. Then she closed her eyes and moved her finger. The rifle kicked violently, and there was a burst of sound. When she opened her eyes, she saw the little red animal lying on its side, torn apart by the furious blast of the buffalo gun. Tears streamed from her eyes as she sank to the ground and stared at the carcass that lay bleeding in the distance. And then she hung her head and pressed her palms down hard against the ashen earth.

She did not know how long she sat on the ground, mourning the death of the fox, but finally she was stirred from her gloom by a noise. She leaped to her feet and yelled a ferocious warning as she rushed forward.

A young man was sneaking up on the carcass and was about to steal it.

Amana hurled herself on his back and knocked him down just as he clutched at the meat. "No!" she shouted. "I swear you will not have it!"

They tossed about on the ground, clawing and biting at one another as they rolled over and over and shouted. The man pinned Amana down and he arched back with a grunt as he lifted his knife. But she twisted out of the way of the blade as it sliced into the ground beside her. With all of her strength she kicked the man in the chest and then staggered to her feet as he screamed with pain and fell back. At once she grabbed for her rifle, but he seized her ankle and pulled her back down on top of him. Somehow she managed to keep hold of the rifle, and as the knife came hissing down into her shoulder, she pulled the trigger and blew the man's face away.

Breathlessly she pulled herself out from under his body. She took up the dead fox in both arms—ignoring the pain in her shoulder—and she staggered toward the camp. She could hardly see. Her legs were trembling. Blood and cinders covered her face and arms. Her hair was matted with dirt and gore from the man's wound. But she continued walking slowly and steadily toward her lodge. When she entered she stood silently in the doorway until Crow Woman approached her and took the meat from her arms. Far Away Son peered at her with tears in his eyes.

"I have . . . brought food," Amana murmured vacantly. And then she collapsed.

When she regained consciousness and opened her eyes again, the sky was lavender and full of sunlight. Many days had passed, and the band's long search for food had ended. The people had finally reached the good hunting grounds where a few buffalo still lingered.

Weasel Woman was dead. Yellow Bird Woman was mad. And SoodaWa was gradually slipping into death as she lay motionless and cold, her breath fading. Amana struggled to get up from the travois that had carried her unconscious body since her injury, and she knelt by her sister and begged her to live. A fragile smile came momentarily into SoodaWa's dark eyes as she gazed steadily at Amana, but she could not move or speak.

In the morning SoodaWa was dead.

More than half the members of the band of Chief Big Belly had also died. The plains reeked with the stench of their decomposing bodies. And those who survived praised the Sun, and they mourned for those who had vanished during that terrible time, which was known among all the peoples of the prairie as the winter of starvation.

Four

For two seasons the people waited for the return of the vast herds of buffalo. With the hot weather, they believed that many of the beasts had strayed into the foothills, climbing to a cooler altitude.

Big Belly was annoyed. "I am too old to be a fool! The buffalo will return. All my life and all the lives of my father and grandfathers there have been buffalo. And there will be buffalo forevermore!" he exlaimed when Amana quietly suggested that perhaps the sacred animals were growing old and dying out.

"Big Belly is right," Far Away Son said, as he smoked with the chief. "Somewhere in the unknown places of the Backbone of the World the animals have been captured by the Cold-Maker. One day Sun will push back the barriers of snow that imprison the buffalo, and they will come back to the prairie."

While the people patiently awaited the return of the sacred beast, they scoured the hills for deer, elk, and antelope. Some game was found by the hunters, but barely enough to keep the families from starving.

Amana worked hard to bring some comfort to Far Away Son and Crow Woman. They were so old that the privation was harder on them than it was on the children and young people. The husband lamented the death of SoodaWa in a long, silent song that sealed him off from the others. He did not speak, and he covered his head with a blanket when he wept. The old woman grieved for her lifelong friend, Weasel Woman; but she nonetheless tried to be of some use. She watched over the skins that Amana had stretched and pegged in the sun, and she patiently and affectionately watched over Yellow Bird Woman when she sat deranged and weeping.

Many of the men had died, and their widows were left to provide for themselves. Their relatives tried desperately to hunt for their greatly enlarged families, but game was scarce and they were weakened by privation. One by one, the old people continued to die.

Though everyone stared when Amana took up her husband's rifle and went out hunting, no one whispered or gossiped about her anymore.

"I don't care what they think," Amana told Crow Woman. "They are helpless. They will starve before they will hunt. They sit silently over empty kettles and dying husbands and crying children! At least my husband has food! And when his heart ceases to mourn, he will come back to his horses. And then he and I together will be hunters!"

Yellow Bird Woman nodded meekly with admiration, hiding her disfigured face behind her hands and gazing in wonder at Amana. "Now you are the most powerful woman in the tribe," she whispered. "Even the men are afraid of you!"

"Well," Amana exclaimed, "I hunt the animals and you and Crow Woman tan the skins. We have meat. And we will even have tea and flour in exchange for the furs!"

When the skins were finally ready for market, Amana packed them carefully on Far Away Son's big mare. Then she drew the mare alongside her pinto, so she would follow its lead. She bid good-bye to her family and started the journey to the trading post that was located northward of the white men's medicine line.

"You cannot go by yourself," one of the elders shouted to her from his lodge. "A woman cannot go alone!"

Amana urged the horses into a gallop and rode quickly over the ridge.

The traders had set up their log house very near the river, instead of among the foothills where they usually built it. But despite the closeness of the trading post to the summer hunting grounds, there were no people and few furs and very little trading.

"It is a hard time for your people," the man said to Amana.

She did not look at him. She never looked into the eyes of white men.

"How much did you bring this time?" he asked.

She pulled the roll of furs from the mare and heaved it into the log house.

"Come in . . . come in. There is no reason for you to stand out there."

Amana ignored the man's remark. She looked at the ground. She kept her hand on her rifle and waited.

"What do they call you?" he asked.

She pretended she did not understand, though the man spoke her language fluently, and she had gradually been learning to speak French from her contacts with the trading post proprietors.

"How come a young woman like you comes in here all by herself?" he muttered while he inspected and counted the pelts. "It's dangerous for a woman," he said.

Still she said nothing. He paused and looked at her impatiently and sighed. "Well, anyway," he said, "somebody should learn how to shoot before they blast away half the value of these skins."

"What do you mean!" Amana snapped. "There is nothing wrong with those furs!"

"Ha! I thought you'd understand me if I said that!" the man exclaimed. "The holes in them furs are the size of frying pans. A good hunter would never blow that kind of a hole in a pelt!"

Amana was visibly shaken. "Well," she muttered, "maybe so . . . but don't try to cheat me. I know about you traders."

The man grinned. "And what is it you know about us?" he chuckled.

"Never mind what I know. Just tell me what I may trade for those furs so I can pack my food and get on my way." She glared into his face for a moment before she returned her glance to the ground.

"All right," he said, "I guess you don't want to be friendly."

"That's right," Amana said. "I just want to trade my furs for tea and flour."

"And how about some of the white man's water? Don't you have some man at home who would like some whiskey?"

"No—no whiskey. We want food. Tea and flour and salt and baking powder. That's all we want—food."

As the man used a big cup to scoop out the provisions for Amana, he kept glancing at her and grinning. "You have a couple of friends just out there waiting for you, don't you?" he said. "Come on—you can tell me. They just send you in because they figure you'll get a better trade, right? And they're watching every move I make right now so if I don't behave myself I'll get my head blown off, right?"

Amana did not answer.

"Well—all right. I always behave myself with you people. You can just tell that to your friends out there." And he chuckled again. "They call me Hugh Monroe. Can you say that?"

Amana ignored the remark.

"Well, anyway, that's what they call me."

Just as the man was bringing the provisions out to Amana, another white man rode up to the post. He was younger and his face did not have hair on it.

The two men talked while Amana quickly loaded the food-filled hide bags on the mare and prepared to leave the post. Then the older one, the man named Hugh Monroe, gestured toward his young friend. "This is *Jean-Pierre Bonneville.* How'd you like that for a name? Almost as bad as some of your Indian names, huh?" And he laughed.

Amana glanced at him resentfully. He acted as if she were stupid; as if she could not understand that he was making fun of her. She disliked him. He smelled like milk, and in his eyes and mouth there was the craziness of whiskey. He chuckled again and she glared at him with undisguised contempt, which only made him laugh the harder. She ignored him, but he kept teasing her. Between his insulting remarks to her he mumbled sly things to the other man in English, which she could not understand. Amana became nervous. The white man with the beard had never acted so badly before when she had come to the post. His manner began to frighten her.

116

But the young man was not laughing. He just kept staring at her intently. Somehow she was not afraid of him.

"Hello," he said very pleasantly, "*o-ke . . . ni-so-koo-wa . . .* greetings, my friend." He looked at her kindly.

"*Mon Dieu!*" the other man exclaimed, clutching his groin and grinning. "*Quelle femme!*"

"*Tais-toi!*" the other one muttered, grabbing his friend by the arm and restraining him. Then to Amana he said: "You should go back to your people now. Perhaps when you come again you will want to talk." And he smiled. "Your people call me *Au-wah-tsahps* . . . screwball." He laughed. "And I am this very drunk and stupid fellow's partner."

Amana stared in bewilderment and felt curiously shy as she mounted and turned her horse into the cottonwood grove that led from the river to the open prairie. She took one last backward look at the handsome young man. And then as he made a waving gesture with his hand, he shouted, "*À bientôt!*"

She galloped away. She rode cautiously upstream under the dense low-hanging cottonwood boughs. And then, where the river made a wide bend away from the trail, she paused briefly on the sandbar to water her horse. For some reason she could not stop thinking about the young man. He seemed kind, as gentle as Far Away Son. She was astonished by the eloquence with which he spoke her langauge, and by the expression of trust that shone in his eyes.

Sunlight filtered through the branches and flitted upon the rushing water that swept the wide, sandy embankment. The warmth of the sun felt good as she relaxed on her horse, thinking about the young man at the trading post.

Then suddenly she heard something.

Without thinking, she reached for her knife. There was somebody in the thicket. She would not allow herself to panic. She pretended she had not heard anything as she watched for a sign of the intruder. Then she saw him. It was the ugly bearded man, creeping toward her through the underbrush.

Amana knew that she would be in great trouble if she killed a white man. No matter her reason, the soldiers in red coats would come looking for her.

For a moment she sat helplessly, watching out of the corner of her eyes as the man with the beard approached her. She started to weep in fear, but then she abruptly shook her head with rage. She would not let herself be abused by this whiskey man! *She would not permit it!*

Without wasting another moment, she leaped from her tranquilly drinking horse and threw herself down on the shore, pulling up her dress and spreading her legs as she pressed handfuls of sand into her groin.

The white man stumbled when he saw what she was doing. "*Oh, sacré!*" he shouted in disgust as he strode to her side and scowled down at her. "What a filthy savage!" he groaned, turning away with repulsion and staggering off.

Amana leaped onto her horse and galloped away. When at last she broke out into the vast openness of the plains, she gave a great whoop and threw back her head victoriously.

As the summer wore on, the elders began to suspect that the buffalo would not return.

"I have gone myself to the agent who speaks for the white men and for the Great Mother across the water, and the agent told me that he had nothing for us. 'Take your people to buffalo and follow the herds,' he said to me. But there are no buffalo, I told him, and many of us are dying."

The councilmen conferred with one another, and decided to move to the river basin, where it was thought buffalo still grazed.

"There may be only a few animals . . . but still we must go. For if we remain here, all of us will perish before winter comes."

The traders followed the tribes wherever they went. They could no longer wait for the people to bring robes and furs to them. The hunting was so poor, and the bands roamed so far from their usual hunting grounds, that the traders had to beg the chiefs to allow them to travel with the starving people.

Near the place called Many Houses, the traders threw up a row of log cabins in the same river valley where the

Piegans had pitched their lodges. Groups of Indian hunters went out in the early morning in search of buffalo. They found nothing.

Far Away Son came out of the lodge as Amana stood silently watching the young men leave the camp. "*Aih*," he said, "it is time that I become a man again. I cannot mourn anymore. Help me with the saddle and get me the rifle, and I will go with them."

Amana hurried away without speaking to carry out her husband's orders. But when she had finished, it was two horses and not one that she had saddled.

Amana did not look into her husband's face as she mounted. "I do not have the strength or the skill for the bow and arrow," she said. "So let me use the rifle."

Far Away Son nodded calmly as he gave his young wife the rifle. Then as he waited patiently for her to return to the tipi for his weapons, Crow Woman came running outside. She was overwhelmed with indignation. "Forbid it, Far Away Son!" she exclaimed. "She will have everyone mocking us again! Stop her from making such fools of us!"

But when Amana was remounted, the old man looked into her eyes with deep admiration and ignored the complaints of the old woman. Amana smiled very faintly and nudged the mare. Instantly the two horses sprang to life and raced in the direction of the party of hunters.

They found buffalo toward the close of the first day out.

From the butte near their camp at the head of a narrow creek, Far Away Son could see that the eastern prairie was black with the burly creatures.

"It is just as Big Belly said—the buffalo have truly returned!" the old man murmured thankfully.

"Hai!" shouted Red Tail, who had ridden up beside Far Away Son and Amana. "Who says the buffalo are gone? It is just as it has always been—the land is dark with them. Never have I seen so many!"

"Perhaps you are right . . ." Amana said dubiously as she peered out into the distance.

"Kai-yo? What is this woman doing here? And what does she know about buffalo? If you don't stop acting like an old fool, and send this crazy wife of yours home where she belongs, we will surely have bad luck!" Red Tail muttered as he waved Amana aside.

"She is a good hunter," the old man said plainly.

"She is a woman!" Red Tail exclaimed.

"She is a good hunter," Far Away Son repeated as he looked calmly at the other man. "Isn't that what matters?"

"Remember how far we have come to find the buffalo!" Red Tail insisted. "Remember that in our homeland in the north, and on the plains in the west, there are none of these precious animals. It is our last chance to remove the blemish that has taken the buffalo from us. Then Sun will accept us as his children once again."

"His children . . ." Far Away Son said very slowly, "the

children of Sun are both male and female. And Amana is a good hunter. She will stay."

Red Tail bounded away in anger.

"That is not the last you will hear of that," Amana warned as she watched after the young man. "He does not like me. And he wishes both of us harm."

Far Away Son chuckled. "Yes, he wishes to harm us because I have a beautiful young wife who turned him away when he tried to talk to her by the river. And then all the girls laughed at him. We all know you sent him running, Amana! Even your old husband heard about it! So I am not surprised that Red Tail is angry to see us. It pleases him to be angry, because once you wounded his pride."

Big Belly was the leader of the party, and the men took orders from him. He led them out on the butte very early in the morning, and after getting a good view of the country and the location of the herds, he decided that the buffalo in the extreme southwest were the most favorable prey.

The dry grass was still tall in these lands beyond the great fires of the previous winter. Instead of cinders and dust, there were grasshoppers and crickets. Small brown birds flitted among the weeds, and the ground was covered with badger holes and heaps of buffalo chips. The lay of the terrain was so favorable to hunting that the party was able to ride to the very edge of the herd before the huge animals became alarmed and began to run.

The buffalo roared. They bounded on their lean legs, carried forward by powerful muscles and the sheer weight of their deep chests, huge heads, and heavy humps. The hunters anxiously awaited a sign from Big Belly. They drew in their horses, who nervously stomped the ground and tossed their heads and tails.

Amana was riding her gentle little pinto. All the way to the hunting grounds she had constantly plied her quirt and called the beast reproachful names in order to keep it beside Far Away Son's spirited mare. But the moment her horse came near the herd it bolted, leaving the hunters behind; rearing up, prancing sideways with arched neck and twitching ears, and then, getting the bit firmly in its teeth, springing out into the chase as madly as any of the best-trained buffalo runners.

"*Ke-ka!*" Big Belly cursed as Amana shot into the herd. Then in exasperation he waved the hunters into action as he glared at Far Away Son.

Now the pinto was faster than Far Away Son's mare. And so he could not easily catch up with his runaway wife. He began to panic as he saw her carried into the avalanche of ferocious, frantically stampeding beasts.

"*Aih! Aih! Aih!*" he shouted as he urged his horse onward. But it was no use; he could not overtake Amana, and his warning shouts and instructions to her were lost in the thunder and rattle of countless hooves.

As Far Away Son hurried toward his wife, he realized that she was not trying to hold in her horse. He could see that she was actually quirting the beast and driving it to run faster! Once she looked back at Far Away Son and she was laughing. Her eyes were shining with excitement. *And she was laughing!*

On she went, over the grassy land and up the slope, until the buffalo scattered among the hunters, who brought them down with a volley of shots.

"What are you doing?" Far Away Son anxiously asked when they drew in their sweating horses. "I was afraid you would fall. I thought you would fall and be trampled. What a fright you gave me!"

Amana was still laughing. "It is so good to gallop free and fast!" she exulted with a wide gesture of her arms. "Just think, Far Away Son, I struck four or five of those beasts with my quirt!"

Far Away Son shook his head in astonishment. Then he too began to laugh.

"I just wanted to keep galloping," Amana sighed. "I never wanted to stop. Nothing frightened me. All I could feel was the power pouring out of me. And so I was unafraid. Once a great big cow buffalo looked up at me as I was riding by and she snorted so hard, I felt her breath on my leg! It was marvelous!"

"What is marvelous," her husband said, "is that you managed not to get killed!"

"And you," Amana asked, "how many of them did you kill?"

"Not one . . ." Far Away Son replied. He hadn't fired a shot, he said; he had noticed absolutely nothing, seen nothing and done nothing. "All I saw was you out there galloping among all those buffalo!" And then he laughed.

They camped that night with Big Belly, whose wife spread out a number of the new buffalo skins and worked steadily on them while visitors came and went. In the latter part of the evening, after the feasting and visiting, Big Belly and Far Away Son sat talking. Big Belly's wife passed around some berry pemmican, and then she nudged Amana and gestured for her to come away from the men and help her with her tasks.

"Every day the young men come back from raiding parties with stories of their attacks against the Crow, or the Assiniboin, or Cree. I think we should also go get some horses from our enemies beyond the Backbone of the World," Big Belly was saying.

"*Aih!*" Amana murmured as she shook herself free of the old wife's grasp and stayed with her husband.

Big Belly leaned close to Far Away Son, and with an expression of delight he whispered: "How would you like to put together a small raiding party?"

"Yes!" Far Away Son and Amana exclaimed together.

Big Belly looked perplexed. He first glanced at Far Away

Son and then he peered at Amana. Finally he said, "I am against this woman's coming with us!"

"Yes, I am against it too," Far Away Son said with a smile, "but she has made up her mind."

"Well, then I just want to repeat that I am against it . . . even though this woman of yours doesn't seem to care what anybody says."

"Then it is decided," Amana concluded happily, as she hugged her old husband.

In the morning about thirty warriors set out under the leadership of Big Belly. They looked innocent enough—as if they were going hunting—for they wore only their plain leggings, skin shirts, and moccasins. But each man also had a bundle tied to his saddle containing his most beautiful war regalia. And in a small cylinder of rawhide they each carried the eagle-plumes or weasel-skin headdress worn by warriors. There was much spirit among the horsemen, who shouted happily to each other as they rode toward the big river.

Amana kept a steady pace with the rest of them. She too had a bundle tied to her saddle, containing the warrior's clothes of grandfather fox. And, though the men ignored her, she was exalted and proud.

After crossing the river into enemy lands, the raiding party carefully concealed itself during the daytime. Wherever the men camped, they kept sentinels posted in positions overlooking the flatland. But there was no sign of anyone in all the vast region, so the camp was peaceful and safe. The fires burned low, and the men smoked.

"*Aih*," Far Away Son sighed one night. "I am getting too old for all this hard riding." And then he crept under a buffalo robe and turned on his side.

Amana pulled down the flap of the lodge and lay down next to her husband. Usually the old man fell asleep almost immediately. But tonight he sighed softly and turned toward Amana. For a very long time he just gazed at her through sleepy eyes. And then he sighed once again and drew back the robe. Amana did not move. "*Aih* . . ." the old man murmured as he looked at his young wife. "What a handsome woman you are," he whispered, lifting her dress and then drawing back so he could lean against the backrest and gaze at her nakedness in the firelight.

"*Aih* . . ."

He did not speak again. He simply sat very quietly, looking tranquilly at Amana's brown body glowing in the half-light of the white coals that filled the lodge with golden shadows.

Amana closed her eyes and felt warm and amorous. She enjoyed the soft sighs of her husband, and for the first time in all the summers she had lived with him, she wanted him to touch her, to lie next to her and press himself against her body. But he did not speak again and he did not touch her. He simply sat before her, looking at her body with an expression of wonder upon his old face.

. . .

The next morning, as they rode toward the foot of a very high butte, they came upon several war houses made of poles, brush, and logs that were so closely laid that even in the darkest night no glimmer of a war party's cooking fire could be seen from the outside.

The raiding party came to a halt and rested and took water while Big Belly sent a scout to the top of the butte. In a very short time he came sliding down the slope as fast as he could move. "A war party is coming this way!" he shouted.

This news caused great excitement.

"They are either Cree or Assiniboin," the scout continued. "They have probably raided the Crow and are hurrying home in fear of pursuit!"

The men laughed and shouted as they rushed for the bundles tied to their saddles, and began to dress for war. Meanwhile Big Belly climbed to the top of the butte. He stood there for a long time, looking out over the plain.

Amana grew anxious. "I don't think he will ever come down here and give us his plan!"

Finally, Big Belly joined his party and said, "They will pass some distance east of here. We will ride down and meet them. If we stay in the coulee they won't be able to see us coming."

Cautiously the raiding party followed their leader down into the dry creek and rode silently toward the approaching enemies. After they had ridden some distance, Big Belly climbed up to the edge of the ravine and peeked out. "We are in their path," he whispered. "When we hear the hooves of their horses, we will all dash up out of here and attack them."

Amana's throat went dry. Suddenly she realized that she was frightened. But when she heard Big Belly give the command, up she went with all the others, out of the coulee and into a cloud of dust.

The enemies and the herd of horses they were driving home were startled by the surprise attack, and the animals stampeded, running between the enemies and the raiding party.

Guns began to fire and arrows filled the air. Amana drew up her rifle. She could feel nothing. She could not think. As she fired, she saw men tumble from their horses and sprawl on the ground. The noise crackled and roared thunderously. Sky and limbs and the terrified eyes of horses spun past her. She felt a great surge in her body and realized that she was shouting.

Then abruptly it was all over.

The enemies had turned and fled in all directions. There was a moment of silence and then all the men began to talk at once. They shouted and laughed and trembled. Amana was overwhelmed. She had been terrified, but once she rode out of the coulee and saw the enemies and their horses, the rifles and feathers and headdresses, she had been filled with strength. Her elegant regalia filled her with strength.

And suddenly her rifle fired. She had fired at several of them, but she was not certain if they had fallen to her shots or those of others in the raiding party.

They had not lost a single man. Only one person was wounded, a youth named Calf Child. Nine of the enemies had died, and fifty of their horses had been taken. Everyone was jubilant. Even Red Tail was happy. He had warned Big Belly that if many men were killed, it would be because of the bad luck brought by having a woman on the raid. But now that they had been victorious, Big Belly laughed and said: "Perhaps this woman warrior brings luck to us!"

It was in that year that the people of the north held many councils and decided to swear allegiance to the Great Mother over the water in the land called England.

"It is a treaty they call by the name *Number Seven* upon which we have put our marks," Big Belly told the people. "And for the lands we have given them, we will receive many good things for all the years to come."

That was the same year that the great chief of the Blood people died. In his place came Chief Three Suns, who was so famous and popular among the bands of the north that Far Away Son told Amana, "At last the time has come for us to rejoin our own Blood tribe and leave the Gros Ventres, with whom we have camped for many years."

And so they ended the summer with sad farewells to Big Belly and his wives. Crow Woman and Amana were anxious to begin the northward journey to the region above the medicine line where the tribe now lived under the supervision of an agent of the Great Mother of England. It was this agent who gave the people food and blankets and many other good things.

Yellow Bird Woman dreaded leaving her own people, despite the contempt they showed her as a woman whose nose had been cut off as a mark of shame. She was afraid of the Blood and begged Far Away Son not to make her go.

"You are a sister to Amana. You are a child of Crow Woman and me. But you are also a Gros Ventre, and if you wish to remain with Big Belly, we will not take you away with us. But, my child," Far Away Son said softly, "how will you live? Who will take in such a woman as you?"

This made Yellow Bird Woman weep.

"I will look after her," the eldest wife of Big Belly agreed as she embraced the sorrowful young woman and bid goodbye to Far Away Son and his family.

Crow Woman kissed Yellow Bird Woman, and then she began to cry and to tremble as she finished packing the travois and got on her horse. Far Away Son called to Amana, for it was already evening and the time for departure had come.

But Amana stood gazing at her friend and she could not come away just yet.

How many summers they had known one another, and

how many marvelous and terrible events had come and gone! Was it possible, Amana wondered, that they could still be the same girls: one so full of love and romance and the other dreaming of heroic adventures and freedom?

"Do not forget poor Yellow Bird Woman," Amana's friend begged, peeking out from behind the scarf with which she covered her face. "Try to think kindly of me. Forgive me for the trouble I have made." And then Yellow Bird Woman shook as if she were consumed by fever. "I am not strong, Amana," she whispered from behind her hands. "I have none of your courage. I had only the courage to love someone once . . . and now look at me. I have suffered because of my love. But Amana, you have dared everything . . . and even though the people gossip about you, they envy you and they are afraid of your great power. How marvelous you are, Amana!"

Yellow Bird Woman wept so violently that she could not speak. But then she seemed to come to life, blooming with an energy that glowed within her heart. "You are one of the holy people, Amana!" Yellow Bird Woman intoned in a clear voice full of power. "I have seen it and I have told all the people. And they have listened to me because I am mad and they know that madness gives me vision," she chanted as she raised her arms and slowly turned in a circle. "Within you, Amana, the spirit of our people lives, and through the legends of your life all of us will be remembered. Believe me, there will be legends, and you will be remembered! Already the many peoples of the plains speak of you. Your name is known in all the places where Sun shines. And the legends of your life are told and retold by people who have never known you, yet one day all of your people will recognize you, Amana. Believe what I tell you, for I have seen it and I know that it will be true! The creatures sing of you and of the great vision they gave you when you were a child. The holy people speak of you. Everywhere I turn I hear songs of you, from the forest and the rivers and the tall grass. So do not forget me, Amana. I am ugly now and I am mad, but do not forget me! It is only through you that I will be remembered!"

The two women embraced. Amana could not speak. She felt afraid, for her heart was so full she feared she might wail with sorrow for her poor friend.

"Do not forget me, Amana," Yellow Bird Woman whispered madly as she withdrew behind her scarf and crouched on the ground.

Amana nodded tearfully, and then she hurried away.

It was during that winter that Far Away Son and his family came back to the ancient homeland of the Blood people. But life was not good there and everything had changed. Where the animals had leaped through the tall grass, there was now a gray land with scattered herds of strange animals called cows, which were the friends of the white men. The creeks that once ran abundantly with good water were soggy with sludge and rust. The air was filled with ash, and the spirits of the trees had abandoned their homes and left only their lifeless, leafless skeletons. The deer had vanished, and so too had the birds of the sky. No glistening white tipis rose against the vast sky; the sky was gray and the tipis were made of canvas. There were no great councils, and all the fires of the Blood Nation had gone out.

The friends whom Far Away Son had known many years earlier had died. They had starved or perished from the sickness or they had been killed by white men and enemy tribes. The old people in whom the power of the Nation lived were gone, and the young were strangers to Amana and Far Away Son. They were unlike any young people they had ever known. For they were full of sorrow and shame. The traders had brought them whiskey and the ministers had brought them a church. And now they were strangers to themselves and to each other.

The agent of the Great White Mother in England no longer cared about the people. He only cared about white men. And if it had not been for the strength of Chief Three Suns, the bands of the north would have had nothing left to them: not land, not freedom, not even the annuities promised to them by treaties.

But Three Suns had a rival named White Calf, and so the life of the Blood people became worse and worse. For now there was a great fight among the people. White Calf had taken his band to the church, and there the minister had made them believe in the white man's god. But Three Suns did not want his people to go to the church and he forbade it.

"Three Suns has many of the people behind him," the elders insisted. "And he is the true leader of our tribe."

Amana and Far Away Son could not understand. They sat silently while the old men shouted at one another.

"White Calf is a dog to the white men. He did not come to council. Instead he went to church. And there he agreed to the loss of our lands. Time after time he has agreed to let them take more and more of our land. And now we have only a small world in which to live!"

"Soon there will be no animals. There will be no Indians. There will be only white men!"

One old man bitterly complained, "White Calf would sell anything to keep his power as chief!"

And so life was not good on the reserve.

"The old ways are being lost," Crow Woman said mournfully as she falteringly placed wood on the fire and then rubbed her gnarled, painful fingers. "No good now . . . with all the young people speaking the white man's language and drinking his whiskey. No good anymore."

Far Away Son sighed but did not speak.

"No good," the old woman continued in a drone, nodding her head and talking to herself. "Now they tell us where to hunt and where to live. They even try to tell us where we have to go after we die. Soon they will put wheels on us like their wagons and just pull us from place to place."

Suddenly a boy stuck his head into the lodge and giggled. "Hey, Amana!" he shouted, "You want to be *ai-in-ai-kiks?* You want to be a policeman?"

Crow Woman shushed the rude child and drove him from the door with a burning stick she drew out of the fire. "You see," the old woman cackled angrily. "No respect! No respect for anybody. The little ones just run around like flies. No good anymore . . . no good."

"The agent," Far Away Son said, "made a society."

"No one will join the warriors' society of a white man!" Crow Woman barked impatiently.

"But they have already joined it," Amana said calmly. "They get some of the money of the Great White Mother for joining. And they also are given a costume to wear."

"So now you want to be a policeman!" Crow Woman complained. "What next? Maybe you will want to be chief!"

"Hush," Amana exclaimed. "You only complain. You have nothing to say anymore unless you are complaining."

"Yes, I am complaining," the old woman continued without taking notice of Amana's displeasure. "I am complaining because everything is full of sorrow. The children speak to the elders without courtesy. No one comes to help me with my water vessel when I go to the creek. The young men just sit in the shade all day, drinking whiskey and doing

nothing. And now even the warriors are becoming police-
men for the white men and telling us what to do and where
to go. Yes, it is true, I am complaining because I have lived
too long. I have lived to see the old ways forgotten."

"Hush, old woman," Far Away Son mumbled. "There
is no use complaining. My head is too full of this sorrow.
I too have lived too long. The hunters are prohibited from
having repeating rifles. The agent says that we may not
have the cartridges for our Winchesters. And only the
sneaking-drink-givers—the whiskey traders—will sell us
ammunition. And they make us give too much for the cartridges because they say the police society will make big
trouble for them if they should get caught." And then Far
Away Son huffed a dry laugh and said, "But they do not
get caught. It is we who get caught by the greed of the
traders."

Amana went to the door and looked into the camp, where
the people were required to live in a gray little flatland
without grass or trees; a sad and neglected place which was
so useless to the white man that he let the Indians keep it.
Mud and trash were piled everywhere, and the air was filled
with the stink of human waste. Of all the vast region that
the Blood had once roamed, this narrow strip of desolate
land was their last home.

The uniformed Indian police made their rounds, herding
the young women and children toward the agency where
the superintendent of the reservation had organized a Sun-

day school. In a little wooden shack he told stories about the white man's god. Amana wanted to hear the stories and she wanted to learn to sing the songs that the people came away singing. But she did not trust the white men.

Crow Woman ranted continually about the changes that had taken place.

"I would rather you dress as a man and join the police society," she exclaimed. "I would rather you were dead than have you listen to the lies of these white men!"

And yet Amana was intrigued by the songs and by all the strangers who visited the Sunday school. She resented the white people and still she was fascinated by the way they dressed and spoke, by the tales they told of another land across the ocean, and the chiefs of many great nations.

"What do these Sunday school Indians call themselves?" Far Away Son asked.

"*Methodists*," Amana answered as she gazed across the settlement where lodges now shared the land with ugly little houses of wood.

"Methodists!" Crow Woman grunted. "What good are they? They are fat and lazy and drunk! So what good are they?"

Amana smiled and kissed Crow Woman. "Get away! Get away! And stop trying to flatter me with all that honey!" the old woman grumbled. "You just want to have your way about this too—as you do about everything else," she snapped. "*Aih!* How sad your poor mother would be if she had lived to see such foolishness! And SoodaWa . . . *Aih,*" the old woman mumbled with a sigh as tears came into her eyes and she rubbed her aching hands together and rocked to and fro before the little fire. "No good anymore . . . no good."

Then Far Away Son took Amana by the hand, and he led her into the sunlight. As they walked through the crowded and littered encampment he murmured, "Do not be angry at Crow Woman. Soon she will be going to Sand Hill. There is nothing left of her life now. The shadow wishes to leave her old body and be free. So be kind to her, Amana."

The shadow that was in Crow Woman's chest gradually strained at her body to be free. The agent said that her ailment was called tuberculosis. But no one knew what to do about it. There had never been such a disease among the people, and all the holy women and medicine men could do nothing to help Crow Woman.

A very old Indian woman much revered for her medicine came to see Crow Woman, but the prayers and herbs did no good.

Another Indian doctor came to see the sick woman, but once again the medicines were of no help. Many holy people came and many tried to cure Crow Woman, but she did not respond to their treatment, and gradually she began to waste away, laboriously gasping for breath and coughing night and day until blood bubbled out of her mouth and nostrils.

Amana waited anxiously for the spring, for surely the warmth of Sun would give her grandmother life. But the winter was long and the snow continued to burden the land with deep drifts. Crow Woman gasped for breath. Far Away Son sat on the couch beside her, his face buried in his hands. The two old people had known each other for many summers. The old woman had been a girl when he was a young hunter. She had been a relative of Amana's mother, and she had always been generous and kind. But despite all of her goodness, now she was dying with blood in her mouth and a look of horror in her eyes.

Amana poured a large bowl of tea and added some sugar to it. The drink seemed to revive Crow Woman. She breathed more easily and she lay back peacefully, without coughing.

"*Aih* . . ." she whispered to Far Away Son, looking with great love into the face of her old friend. "I think perhaps it is better . . . I think maybe it is good that I vanish with the world I knew."

"Hush," Amana murmured as her husband turned away in sorrow and covered his face.

"It is all right," the old woman said calmly, looking high into the sky where the clouds rose above the smoke hole. "I do not want to see this life . . . I do not want to see my people fading away day by day. I would rather be free of this bad life. I would rather remember the land as it was when I was a girl: when each tree told me its secret and the animals gave us power and vision. I would rather remember the good days when the Cold-Maker brought the snow and Sun blessed us with abundance and freedom. That is what I would like to remember."

Far Away Son began to sing very softly. His wheezing old voice brought a faint smile to Crow Woman's lips. She nodded her head and sighed contentedly. But even before the song was ended, a dark stream began to flow slowly from her mouth: the last, terrible hemorrhage.

The smile lingered even after the intense light in Crow Woman's eyes went out.

Crow Woman died in the spring, during the year that the surveyors for the Canadian Pacific Railway swarmed into the region and began to lay out the long lines for the tracks that would transform the ancient homelands of the Blood into an alien nation. The Indian people of the north did not want the railroad, but still it came to them, making a trail from Medicine Hat to the northern edge of the reservation. And then, one winter's day, when Amana was talking about going in search of the last remaining buffalo, the fire wagon made thick smoke and great thunder as it came stumbling down the tracks for the first time, hooting and growling and sending the precious game running in every direction.

"It is a good thing . . ." Far Away Son murmured as he stood staring in astonishment at the apparition puffing and groaning before him, "it is truly a good thing that Crow Woman did not live to see this monster of the white man. She would have known that the days of our people are gone. Like the buffalo and the deer, we are being driven out of our land. Soon there will be nothing to eat. Soon there will be nothing left but memories."

The next day Eagle Plume called upon nine men to go with him to hunt a small herd of buffalo that was reported to be just south of the reservation.

"If we do not go now the fire wagons will scare them away forever, and then we will starve as the winter grows colder," he told his friends. "And so," Eagle Plume continued, "I have asked only our very best hunters to accompany me."

"But you have not asked me," Amana exclaimed as she approached the men with her rifle in hand. "And I am as good a hunter as all the rest of you."

"That is true," Far Away Son said as he accompanied his young wife into the circle of men. "You must be fair and agree that Amana has proven herself a fine hunter and warrior."

"*Aih!*" Eagle Plume shouted angrily. "I have tolerated a woman on our raids in respect to you, Far Away Son. I have voiced no objection as long as it was your wish that Amana accompany us and as long as you yourself rode with us. But now you are too old for hunting. And we will not take your wife with us if you cannot come too."

The men nodded and spoke out in agreement.

"Then," Far Away Son said very calmly, "I will have to ride with you, because I could not allow you to pay my wife so grave an insult. She has fed many of you when you were too weak to find your own food. She has ridden beside you, and she has captured many horses. And I cannot believe that the white man's religion in which you now believe and the white man's whiskey that you now drink has made you forget how to respect a good hunter and warrior."

Far Away Son's words disgraced the men, and they stood silently looking at one another in shame. "Even if you disapprove of Amana as a woman," he concluded with an eloquent ring in his voice, "you must respect the great vision that gave her power and made her such an exceptional woman!"

The men nodded their agreement and urged Eagle Plume to allow Amana to accompany them.

"Only if her husband will take charge of her," the old warrior insisted.

"Then I will do so," Far Away Son agreed.

So Far Away Son and Amana prepared their horses and weapons and were soon ready to depart.

By the next day they had arrived in the vicinity of the small herd of buffalo. Though it was bitterly cold, the sun shone brightly on the hard-packed ground. The hunters were in the best of spirits as they sprang onto their horses and raced into the midst of the surprised animals.

Amana thought of nothing but proving once again that

she was as good a hunter as any of the men. She gave all of her energy to hunting down a fat cow. She did not want the meat or robe so much as she wished to silence all doubts about her abilities.

With each well-aimed shot, she brought down one sturdy cow after another. And when she finally stopped, she found herself alone.

She looked back urgently, searching for Far Away Son. People were gathered in a little group far behind her. And from this cluster of hunters came a long, frail wailing sound.

Amana shouted in dread and rage as she galloped toward the huddled figures, still searching the horizon for some sign of Far Away Son. When she reached the men, she leaped from her horse, threw down her rifle, and broke into the crowd.

Then she sighed with relief. Two Bows had been thrown from his horse and his leg was broken. But he was already being helped, and he was laughing proudly despite his injury.

Only after Two Bows had been carefully carried to his horse did Amana notice the four hunters who still clustered over another body. When the men saw Amana peering at them they turned away in shame and sorrow and they wept for her.

It was Far Away Son.

He had been charged by a huge old bull. Wounded and mad with pain, the great beast had lunged into Far

Away Son's horse, tearing out its flanks and knocking Far Away Son to the ground. He had been trampled by the running herd of buffalo.

"Do not look at him, Amana," a young man pleaded. "He is no longer your husband."

But Amana pressed silently through the arms of the men who restrained her. She silently looked down at the sunlit blood that drenched the broken heap of flesh and bones. Then in a daze she turned away.

She could not think. She could feel nothing. Suddenly everything in the world had vanished. All that remained was a huge storm of bright sunlight and emptiness.

"Now," she muttered in a dry whisper, ". . . now I am truly alone."

Amana drew the breath of life into her breast as she wept.

The great white gust of air filled her with infinite sorrow and regret. In the wind came the long lonely songs of the dead stretching endlessly behind her. She sat alone, holding the gleaming severed locks of her hair in both hands, staring into the emptiness of the shadows that came with the winter. Nothing moved. Nothing was born and nothing grew. There was only the long lean torrent of a deathly gale full of dead voices.

Then from a distance came a small sound. Amana stirred

and her face momentarily filled with excitement. But the sound faded and the tears came back into her eyes.

The desolate plain fell into a terrible silence. The moon came slowly into a pitiless sky. Dust twisted aimlessly over the trampled grass where the lodges had once stood. Now the people were gone. There was no one left to befriend Amana. She had no family. No hunter who would take her into his family. No father or sister or brother. And so she sat alone, waiting for the wolves as the moon arose into the unpeopled night.

She was thinking of SoodaWa and Far Away Son and Yellow Bird Woman, of the grandmothers and of her mother and father. She was thinking of all the love that had vanished with those precious people of her life. And the thought filled her with such sorrow that she cried out for a sign that the good days had not gone forever. She begged the sky for a sign that she would survive, that she might once again raise herself with the vision that had been given to her so many long years ago.

Then, again, a distant sound!

Amana stood up abruptly and urgently listened. For a moment it seemed as if that friendly noise in the utterly silent world had evaded her. But then, she heard it once again. She gasped with delight, and she wept as she recognized the small song that crept feebly from the throat of the earth.

"I am your vision," it said. "I am the seed that grows. I

am the cave of your heart and the drum that summons legends and dreams!"

"*Aih!*" Amana exclaimed, as she opened her arms to the night and began to run into the deep darkness that stretched beneath the vast beadwork of the sky.

Far out in the meadow, beyond the brown grass and the dead trees, a bright-red creature ran unnoticed into the stars.

It was a fox! Sniffing the dark land that Old Man had made—where the ceremonial fire still burned and where we cast our tiny shadows against a gigantic sea of human dream and memory.

"Yes . . ." Amana murmured with a gentle smile as she ran into the deep night. "It is a fox!"